KATHARINE MURRAY

THOMAS NELSON PUBLISHERS
Nashville • Atlanta • London • Vancouver

Published in Nashville, Tennessee, by Thomas Nelson, Inc., Publishers, and distributed in Canada by Word Communications, Ltd., Richmond, British Columbia.

Library of Congress Cataloging-in-Publication Data

Murray, Katharine.
    Jake / Katharine Murray.
    p. cm.
    "A Jan Dennis Book."
    ISBN 0-7852—8095-2
    I. Title.
PR6063.U739J3   1995
823'.914—dc20   994-31892
                                   CIP

1 2 3 4 5 6 — 99 98 97 96 95 94

Contents

Skipping

1

Jeanie had skipped school the day she first met Jake. From the field behind the bungalow she watched the school bus arrive, stop to pick up its only other passenger from the village, and roar off asthmatically down the road. She waited, half-hidden behind the overgrown holly bush at the corner of the garden fence, until she was quite sure nobody was around to see.

Here on the outskirts of the village where their house stood in a rectangular bite taken out of a vast cornfield, there were no neighbors to peek from behind silk curtains. Even passersby were rare. But you never knew . . . secrets, in Sea Norton, England, were impossible to keep.

A final nervous glance over her shoulder, and Jeanie wrapped her blazer carefully around her schoolbag and leaned over the low fence to push the bundle down behind the overgrown shrubs at the back of what had once been a flower bed. With her head still bent she took a furtive upward glance at the bungalow windows. As she had expected, the faded curtains between the blistered paintwork of the windows still hung limply closed.

She had never done it before. Not for the lack of

opportunity, but because it was not her nature to rebel, however bad things had been. Up to now, somehow she had managed to grit her teeth and hang on. Even today her own daring made her insides knot and churn. It took an effort to turn her back on the house and let her eyes rest on the morning landscape, where a dark, trodden path bisected the stubble field. September haze lay silkily over the flat land. Spiders had threaded the hedgerows with a million beads of sun-caught dew. She took in a deep breath of cool air, feeling the touch of sea-smelling wind on her face. It was hopeless trying to go on the way things were. Today—just this one day, no matter what the consequences—she, Jeanie, had to be free.

She skirted the village in a wide circle, scrambling through gaps in fences and avoiding the wide open spaces. When in the distance somebody called a dog, she froze in the shadow of an empty barn, watchful. No one appeared. She went on.

The farther she walked, the more the tight knot of fear in her stomach unravelled and ran away into unreality. What could they do to her, after all? A small smile crossed her face at the thought. Daring even more, she tried a bolder one, "I don't care what other people say." She said it to herself in a whisper, and the freedom seemed to run through her veins, bringing a little spring unnoticed into her gait. Forget school, she said to herself. Forget Mom, even. This is my day, all my own.

As she neared the coast a massive rampart of sanddunes, bristling with coarse green grass, blotted out the sky. In the damp pass between dunes, beds of rushes rippled and whispered. The village was behind her now. The beach road, running straight as a die from the crossroads to the sea, cut through the dunes, ending in a concrete slipway on the beach. Next to it a square hut, where the inshore lifeboat was kept, stood guard at the sea's gate.

Jeanie paused and looked around carefully before crossing the gap. Between tidy rows of holiday bungalows the road was empty, salted with a fine scattering of windblown sand. Far away outside the shop a post office van stood, scarlet as poppies. A tiny figure moved towards it. Too far away to see.

She stopped to take off her shoes and socks and clambered to the top of the dune, feeling the cool sand slip between her toes and the grass roots prick and tickle. Since she was tiny she had loved that feeling, mixed with anticipation of afternoons spent on the beach, Dad and Mom and her. Long-ago afternoons.

At the top the full strength of the salt wind met her, whipping the long dark hair across her face. Shivering, as the chill of it blew through her jumper and blouse, she stood her ground, breathing in deeply, letting it cleanse away the lurking shreds of guilt. *Today is mine*, she said to herself again, *today I am not responsible for anything, today I don't have to brace myself until it hurts, and struggle on.*

Inland, the tall crenellated tower of the church gathered the village roofs around its tree-clad skirts. Beyond, traffic rushed gleaming north and south along the coastal route, and beside it sat the distant cube of home. Below, almost at her feet, hippies had grouped a clutch of battered buses and vans in the dune's shadow, half-hidden by scrubby willow and alder bushes. The smell of wood smoke drifted up and was snatched away by the wind, and with it the thin sound of a baby crying. A sudden chorus of dogs barked and were silent again.

Decisively now, Jeanie turned towards the sea. The broad sandy beach stretched away on either side as far as she could see, the distance measured off by sand barriers pointing to the horizon. Not a soul in sight, not even a boat far out to sea. No one to spoil it for her. On a sudden wild impulse she spread her arms and, yelling, swooped like a seagull down off the dunes, across the wet sand and, gasping with the cold, into the restless waves.

Later, she climbed back up to the top, dragging her feet in the warming sand to dry them. Deliberately she turned her face away from home, setting off northward up the meandering coastal path. Sometimes the path ran along the top of a single ridge between the flat fields and the sea; then in places the dunes would divide and multiply into a complex range of wind-built hills and valleys. Then the path would dip and climb, now turning away from the sea, now twisting back to regain it. She walked for an hour in the strengthening sun. It was a long time since she had walked so far, and she had had no breakfast. The ups began to tire her. Finally, she settled her back against the warm sand in a sheltered hollow and rested. Slowly she felt her body let itself be cradled. It felt good. She had not slept much last night. Her eyes closed.

When she opened them again, Jake was there on the ridge above her. Like a scarecrow outlined against the sky, his long coat streaming in the wind, he stood still, hands in pockets, head thrown back, staring out to sea, like a powerful echo of herself. Was she dreaming him? She shook her head to make sure she was awake, and the slight movement must have caught in his eye. He dropped his gaze from the horizon and began to pick his way down the slope towards her.

Closer to her now, he was even more scarecrowlike. Very tall and thin, and dressed in a collection of ancient garments which had been meticulously patched and darned, apparently with the remnants of even older ones. Jeanie kept still in her hollow, unsure whether he had seen her, unsure, out of habitual wariness, whether she wanted to be seen.

She was not frightened, in spite of the warning bells about strange men ringing loudly in her head. No one could be frightened of Jake. He had nothing of that predatory air that she recognized in some and knew to beware of. Even when he came closer—carefully, and not too close, so as not to alarm her—instinct reassured her that, strange as he was, she was safe with him. Later she told herself that from that first moment she had loved and trusted him.

"Hello," he said—and then waited, saying nothing else. Not demanding any explanation, but seeing everything: her sea-stained schoolgirl-gray skirt and jumper, the shoes dangling from her hand, the look of mixed exhaustion and elation in her eyes.

Jeanie stood up slowly, giving herself time. His face was still a long way above her—a thin, bony face with dark hair flopping over it and a stubbly beard clinging to its cheeks. His eyes were what she noticed most—dark brown, humorous, and gentle.

With an effort she gathered all her dignity around her. She had started this day being true to herself, and this person was not going to make her ashamed. She thought he didn't want to. For once, Jeanie had no wish to hide.

Her words came out all tumbled because she wanted him to understand.

"I'm supposed to be at school. But I'm not there today because I can't . . . "

And then it all came back. Everything that had happened since *that day*. Robert Wylie turning away with that awful expression of pity and bewilderment. Caroline Adamson whispering with her group of hangers-on. The conversations that ended when she came into the classroom. Sitting beside an empty seat on the bus day after day after day. Then the notes left in her desk, in her locker, in her pockets after PE, following her wherever she went.

She was shaking all over, shaking violently—teeth chattering, legs turning into jelly, sliding, slipping, falling. She felt Jake's hands gently reach out and hold her before everything went black.

Her first awareness with returning consciousness was of the roughness of his coat wrapped around her. She was cold, apart from a horrible familiar warm clamminess around her thighs. Then: Oh no, not again, it's happened again. Tears of exhaustion and self-pity trickled from underneath her eyelids.

"It's all right." His voice was soft and dark brown like his eyes. "You're epileptic, aren't you? Don't worry, I know how to look after you. I was a nurse once. It's a good thing I was here. You've pushed yourself a little too far."

She tried to nod her head, but the muscles would not

obey her. Her whole body felt strange, not belonging to her. The voice went on, not waiting for an answer, tranquil, unhurried, soothing as a lullaby.

"Don't try to talk. You're too tired. I'm going to carry you back to where I live. Just relax. It's going to be all right."

She knew she trusted him. For the first time in a very long while she could let go, let somebody else take charge of everything. She closed her eyes, and with a long sigh let him lift her and carry her up the dune.

In spite of his emaciated look, his arms were strong. Rocked by the rhythm of his stride, she leaned into his chest, feeling at home. Not since Dad died . . . He seemed to carry her a long way. She drifted on the borderline of wakefulness, confused between reality and dreaming, until she felt herself put down, a pillow adjusted under her head, a blanket pulled over her. Then the long slide down into sleep.

A Dancing Day

2

arla woke that morning to the sound of the dogs barking. At once, before her eyes opened, her other senses sprang to attention. The dogs' chains rattled as they strained to reach something passing by on the dunes above the encampment. Another dog? A fox late back to its earth? People seldom used the footpaths near the camp. Most of the villagers would go a long way around to avoid the travelers. Carla was used to people crossing the road to avoid her, acting as if she was not there. Those who suddenly, for no reason, hurled abuse were harder to ignore. The only way was to clamp down hard inside on the red fury they aroused.

The dogs' racket subsided and Carla stretched back luxuriously. Splinters of sunlight scattered across her blanket from the cane blind at the window. She held out a naked arm to see the morning light gild the reddish down on her freckled skin, turning it this way and that, laughing softly to herself, in no mood for angry thoughts. It must be late, but what did it matter? She lay still a while, listening, picturing, tasting the feel of the new day. Sun. Wind whistling through the grass on the dunes. Racing clouds in the sky, spume on the wave-tops. A day for dancing.

She drew her knees up to her chin and in a single graceful movement kicked off the covers and stood upright in the narrow space beside her bunk bed.

A dancing day. Rummaging in a box of clothes pulled out from under the bunk, she found a long turquoise skirt and a frothy petticoat. A white vest, an emerald scarf tied gypsy-wise over her mass of bright red hair, and she was ready. She laughed mockingly at herself in the mirror and slid back the plywood partition that separated the tiny room she shared with her younger sister from the main section of the bus.

The remains of the family's breakfast lay on the folding table. She paused, head tilted a little to one side as she played her private game of placing each person by the sounds that came through the open door. The intermittent thump of her father splitting firewood. The tiny clicks of Mom's lace bobbins from her favorite seat by the bus door. Distantly, the shrieks of little Gwennie and David tobogganing on the duneside. And Owen? Off after rabbits, Carla decided. He had said as much last night. She cut a slice of bread from the loaf in its scatter of crumbs, poured a mug of milk, and stepped outside with her breakfast in her hand.

A dancing day. A sky pale blue like a thrush's egg, a mellow sun already drying the dew from the bowed grass stems. Carla danced up the slope and lay in her particular spot overlooking the sea, chewing and feeling the song of the waves flow through her veins and make her toes tap to their own wild rhythm.

Someone was there, on the beach. Someone Carla had seen before. That odd, frail-looking girl from the village. Noticeable because she seemed an outsider—always alone, always scurrying about errands, always hunched as if the cares of the world were on her shoulders. But not now. Now she was rushing at the waves and jumping over them like a wild child, shrieking and laughing when they splashed her. This girl obviously shared her private feeling of what today was for.

But Carla knew she would not be welcome to join her. This was a private dance. She kept still, watching intently as Jeanie left the shoreline and clambered into the dunes. She noticed the school-gray skirt and blouse, the air of mixed nervousness and determination as she set off up the path. Then Carla rolled over to look into the endless vault of the sky above her. Thank goodness I'm free, she thought. Thank goodness I don't have to be shut up in school on a day like this.

She liked this stopping-place on the East coast, tucked in behind the mountainous sanddunes on a pocket of land that nobody seemed to own. At least the villagers left them alone, and once the holiday season was over they had the shore mostly to themselves. They would stay another month, perhaps, until the caravan site up the track closed down for the winter, cutting off their water supply. Then it would be back to Wales, to their old wintering spot on the farm with potatoes to be picked, back to the cold and mud of another winter, back to the school where she never really belonged. She turned her mind away.

A shadow blotted out the sun. Her brother Owen had come silently, barefoot, along the path and stood looking down at her in his quiet detached way. A couple of snared rabbits swung from their heels. Carla sat up, squinting against the sun.

"A good catch?"

He shrugged. "Not bad. They're only babies, but they'll make a stew."

Carla looked distastefully at the rabbits' mangled necks, at the blood clotting the soft fur. Sentimental, Dad called her, when she went outside rather than see them skinned. The natural world isn't all peace and beauty, he would say, it's full of things destroying and being destroyed, and we're just a part of it. We don't disrupt the harmony by using what nature provides. She looked away. Down on the beach a herring gull was smashing a crab against the post of one of the breakwaters. Suddenly the morning didn't seem so lovely any more.

"Where did you go?" she asked Owen, to distract herself.

He jerked his head northward. "Plenty of rabbits on the dunes. They dig holes in the sand. I can find their runs easily. Only these two from a dozen snares, though. Must be getting wary of me. I'll try the other way tomorrow."

He paused, staring thoughtfully out to sea. "I saw this girl on my way back. I ducked behind a ridge, she didn't see me. Walking up the dunes as if someone was after her. Odd-looking girl. . . "

"I know who you mean," Carla broke in eagerly. She began to tell Owen about Jeanie, how she had seen her in the village, how she had been dancing in the waves.

But Owen was already pulling a knife out of his

pocket, slithering down in the sand to gut his catch and wash them in the sea. People did not fascinate him, especially those who did not belong to their way of life. The world of plants and animals was far closer to his heart.

Carla closed her eyes and saw Jeanie as she had seen her for the first time, coming out of the shop with a bagful of groceries. She was tiny, pale, and birdlike, her eyes enormous, her long hair hanging over her face like a curtain drawn on the world. Her fragility made Carla ache painfully with the desire to protect and heal—like the pathetic draggled fledglings she often tried, and failed, to save from dying.

As Jeanie crossed the road the handle of her bulky bag snapped, and suddenly potatoes and oranges and multi-colored cans were rolling wildly in all directions. She stood there, head hanging, staring at a box of eggs oozing yolklike yellow pus, as if without the strength to pick them up.

Across the road on the churchyard wall a trio of youngsters—two young men in jeans and leather and a pretty girl—watched her silently. Usually they had plenty to say, insults, banter, the usual more or less good-tempered noise. Carla, used to their kind, could give as good as she got. But Jeanie, they just watched. Their silence sent a shudder down her spine.

Deliberately, Jeanie turned her back on them and began with enormous effort to gather up the scattered things. Carla found a can of beans that had rolled away along the gutter and handed it to her, smiling with all her might, longing to give her a crumb of comfort. Never mind that bunch over there, she wanted to say, you're worth twenty of them. Jeanie took the can without looking up. A moment later, her arms wrapped protectively around the broken bag, she turned to walk down the road, her upright back as rigid as a crucifix.

The group on the wall stared her out of sight. Carla too stood and stared, until one by one the heads turned, taking stock of her. Deliberately, she spat in the dust. The tall fair boy, the handsome one, the ringleader, inspected her slowly as if she was a particularly revolting piece of trash. His lip lifted in a contemptuous smile that was more like a snarl. She knew he hated her.

She couldn't forget Jeanie. It was as if she knew her. How stupid, she told herself, when they inhabited different worlds. Only Jeanie didn't seem to belong in hers, not with the spick-and-span hedged-in life of the village, not with the tight-lipped disapproval of the woman in the shop who served the travelers as if it hurt her to breathe the same air. Carla might flare up with anger, but in the end she could always turn her back and not let it bother her. It didn't matter, she had another world to go to. But what if you had nowhere else to belong, and your own people didn't want you?

It must hurt to be Jeanie, Carla thought. She could see how Jeanie held everything inside and made herself go on.

"The world is full of conflict, and we have to make it work for us, not fight against it. In nature, one creature thrives on the destruction of others, and everything is renewed through death and decay." She heard her father's voice speaking slowly in the firelight as he loved to do, sitting late under the stars. Carla would lean warm and comfortable against her mother, listening lazily. Dad seemed to have it all worked out, everything made sense when he talked about it. But his way of thinking took no account of Carla's anger. Surely, she raged inwardly, people are different. Do we have to be part of the inevitable cycle, destroy and be destroyed, fight and kill and drive each other away? Don't we have a choice?

Carla sighed so deeply it was almost a sob, and sat up from the dune, pushing the hair out of her eyes. Her fingers hurt. She had angrily dug hard into the sand, driving particles of grit deep under her nails. The sky was still clear and blue, but the dancing was over now. She determined to do something to take her mind off things.

The tide was ebbing. Time to see what it might have brought in. Automatically she began to scan the dark line of debris at the high-water mark, picked out a larger object in the distance, and headed towards it, lifting her skirt up to keep it from blowing in the wind.

Jake's House

3

Jeanie emerged from sleep. Fragments of a strange place floated into focus and floated out again. Rough planks and rafters above her. Through a small window, dusty sunlight. Wooden walls. A table with an oil lamp, a kettle and a battered stove. A shelf with packets of food, a pile of books.

Then Jake, sitting on a bench against the opposite wall, sewing. She watched him secretly, cocooned in a comfortable weakness, not ready, yet, to face whatever came next. He worked quickly and deftly, his long sensitive fingers handling the needle with confidence. A wisp of dark hair hung over the nape of his neck. She would have liked to touch that neck . . . The thought astonished her, sending a surge of intense happiness and longing through her whole body. It must have startled her into a smile, because when Jake looked up he smiled in return.

"Feeling better? You've been asleep for a couple of hours." He held up what he had been stitching: an extremely faded pair of jeans with dark green patches. "I'll have these finished in a minute. You'll want to change and get your things washed. I've taken in the waist, and there's a belt somewhere." He bent and rummaged in a wooden box on the floor beside him.

Jeanie was glad his face was hidden as her warm content was violently overtaken by a cold sweat of embarrassment. She had wet herself. At fifteen years old! And he knew. It was horrible. The doctor had told her it would happen, that she couldn't help it, but every time she still felt dirty, humiliated, and ashamed. She couldn't look up at Jake as he dropped the jeans lightly on the bed and went to the door.

"There's some water and a towel over there. Take your time. Let me know when you're ready, and I'll make us a cup of tea."

He was a good tailor. Once the legs were rolled up, the jeans fit well enough. She felt better, clean and dry. Dropping her stinking pants and skirt into the bucket of water, Jeanie picked it up and opened the door.

Immediately she recognized the place. The long grass and gnarled apple trees were part of the old orchard at the back of Seymour Place. Dad used to bring her here when she was little, to see old Mr. Seymour and his regiment of cats. She remembered crawling through the undergrowth on an afternoon just like this, following a ginger kitten who led her on in playful darts and rushed, always just out of reach. The hut—she stepped outside and looked up at it—yes, it was here that the kitten had found a refuge perched on a stack of fenceposts and rolls of chicken wire, out of reach, all fur and ears and heartless golden eyes.

Mr. Seymour had died years ago, the land was sold, the house mouldered away. Nobody came here any more.

Dad had brought her . . . Blinking sudden tears away,

Jeanie looked for Jake. He was sitting under one of the apple trees, placidly doing something with a knife and a piece of wood.

"I need some more water."

"Tap's over there." He jerked his head sideways. She was glad he did not offer to help, that she could wade alone with her burden through the long grass between the trees. Ten yards farther on was a wire fence; on the other side of it, a cattle-trough with a rusty tap. She wrung out her clothes as best she could, swilled out the bucket and refilled it. Her muscles still felt weak and rubbery. Hanging up her clothes on a length of rope stretched between two trees, she felt the cleansing breeze take them with relief. She would be able to face him now.

Ducking out from under the last of the low branches, she paused to consider the old hut. He had been working on it. Pale new planks lined the walls, the putty around the window was fresh. The roof, though sagging, was watertight with new roofing tiles. Even a garden plot had been reclaimed from the tangled undergrowth. In Jake's sitting place, a salvaged fish crate under the tree, the ground was worn with use.

Jake actually lived here. She had to adjust the way she saw him. His wild and windswept appearance on the dune had made her think of him like an exotic migrant bird brought in by autumn gales, belonging to another world. Just some kind of tramp, she supposed. A kind man who had happened by at the right moment to help her, she told herself firmly. She needed to be firm, because something very strange was happening inside her. She felt as if fate had sent a knight in shining armor galloping into her life on a white horse to sweep her completely off her feet.

She took a deep breath and walked steadily towards the open door of the hut.

"Tea?"

Jake took a steaming kettle off the stove on the table and poured water into a tin pot. Jeanie sat on the bed and gratefully accepted a large mugful.

"Hungry?"

She nodded. The day was well on, and she had not eaten. Jake fetched a loaf of bread from a biscuit tin on the shelf and began to cut thick slices, spreading them with butter from a chipped dish and chunks of yellow cheese. Jeanie watched him, slowly unwinding in his comfortable silence. It was true. He was just a nice, ordinary man—and for some reason she did not understand, she desperately wanted to tell him all about herself.

"My name's Jeanie," she burst out, and went on urgently, before he could respond.

"I live in the village with my mom. Dad died two years ago, and Mom hasn't been the same since. The doctor says she's depressed. She doesn't do anything, except on good days. I have to look after her. And the cooking, and the house—it's all right, I can do all that. But I wish Mom . . . " She stopped short. Even to him, she couldn't talk about that.

"Four months ago I started having these fits. The doctor at the hospital says I won't have any more when they get the drugs right for me, but it takes time. I have to keep seeing him and having tests. I had a fit at school and I, I wet myself, and ever since then nobody'll have anything to do with me. Mostly they didn't like me anyway, but there was one, and even he . . ."

Again she stopped. That hurt too much too.

"Then some of them ganged up on me. It got to be too much. I couldn't face school this morning."

She finished lamely, looking down at the fingers twisting nervously in her lap. She had ended up trying to make an excuse, when she had really wanted to explain how things were. But Jake just smiled and nodded gently, and went back to his task making a neat sandwich, cutting it in four pieces and arranging it on a cracked plate with as much care as if it had been bone china. Then, deliberately, he stood and made her a formal bow across the table, handing her the plate with a flourish like a butler with a silver serving tray in some lofty baronial hall. Only the mischievous gleam in his eyes betrayed him.

"Pleased to meet you, Jeanie," he said gravely. "My name is Jake."

His clowning burst the bubble of tension in a shower of laughter. She couldn't help it. She laughed and laughed, she doubled up until she ached with it. She laughed at him, at herself, at her own laughter, and eventually because it was just so good to laugh. And Jake laughed with her—a deep, rich, uninhibited, childlike laughter, that seemed to bubble up from joy itself.

Slowly the tide ebbed. Jeanie wiped her streaming eyes, feeling weak but oddly light, as if a weight had rolled off her back. It was so long since she had laughed like that. As she sat up, her hunched and rounded shoulders straightened, her head came erect and, for the first time, she looked Jake full in the eye.

"That's better," Jake said softly, startling her into awareness of what she had just done.

How can he know me so well? The thought shot through her mind and frightened her so much that she almost turned and ran. Then, as she looked at him, that powerful, pleasurable happiness flowed over her again, and she knew that she couldn't run now because she loved him. This was what it was, being in love. Even though she hardly knew him, Jake was the most wonderful, the most extraordinary person in the world, and from now on the most important thing in her life was being near him. Nothing would ever be the same again.

Looking up into Jake's eyes, she felt her insides melt with love. He was still smiling. She knew that, incredibly, he accepted her. He even liked her. Even if he didn't love her the way she loved him, he was never going to tell her to go away. He wasn't that kind of man.

Suddenly she wanted to start all over again, telling even the things that had been too painful to say before. She began at the beginning again, pausing only for ravenous bites of sandwich and quick gulps of tea. She told him how sometimes she felt all alone in a black hole, with no way out, no one to call for help. She talked about the invisible walls that seemed to exist between her and the rest of the world. About the day two years ago when Dad went out in the car and never came back. How Mom ceased to be Mom, and she had had to learn to be strong for both of them. About the cool, clinical world of doctors and social workers, who used long words and went away again.

Jake made her another sandwich, refilled her mug, and she went on.

She tried to describe the daily struggle to keep Mom going, to try and get her to cook and clean and wash and shop, to make sure the bills were paid and that someone answered the door when the milkman called. It was so hard to keep up the semblance of normality so that people would believe they were all right, so that they wouldn't take her away and put her into foster care.

If it hadn't been for the epilepsy, things might still have been all right. She had even, at last, found a friend— Robert Wylie, a shy boy at school, slow to make friends, laughed at for being clumsy and wearing thick glasses. They had drifted together, two odd ones out, spent their lunch hours side by side in an out-of-the-way corner of the school grounds. He too had problems at home. Slowly, they had begun to be able to talk.

Even for Robert, seeing his friend jerking in a fit in a pool of her own urine was too much. As she came to, she had seen him turn away, shuddering. Since then he had avoided her.

Jake listened, very quiet and still. When words were no longer enough and dissolved into wrenching, painful sobbing, he found a handkerchief, and then another one, and waited patiently until she had finished. Jeanie felt exhausted, bled dry of misery, but wonderfully separate from it all, as if she could step back and look at her life and say, "It's all been awful, but look at me, I've survived." She put her head down on her arms on the table, and let the peace wash over her.

When she opened her eyes Jake was not there. The

sun was shining brightly through the open door. It must be well into the afternoon.

He came through the orchard and up the steps with her clothes.

"Your mother will be looking for you."

Jeanie sat up and smiled at him, then stretched luxuriously, not in a hurry to go, noticing how the thought of Mom did not worry her.

"She doesn't take much notice of time. But I ought to go home and cook dinner."

He walked with her up to the old house and said good-bye in the lane. Suddenly being alone again frightened her. She didn't want to leave him. She wanted to stay here with Jake, she wanted to throw her arms around his neck and be held close and safe. She thought she saw a flicker of warning in his eyes, the hint of a frown, as he caught and interpreted her look. Then he smiled, the crinkly, friendly smile she already knew so well.

"Can I come again?"

"Of course. Whenever you like."

"You'll still be here? You're not going away?"

For a moment Jake did not reply. Then he looked at her very straight and hard and said something strange.

"I go where the wind blows. When I arrive, there's always a place for me. Just now it's here, but next month, next year, it could be somewhere else. It all depends on the wind."

Then he was gone, leaving Jeanie staring after him. She saw him again, vividly, as she had first seen him, high on the dune, windblown, far and free like a sea gull, soaring. What did he mean? The way he spoke, it was as if it was something important. Was it just that she must never think she could own or hold onto him? Or was it more than that, something she couldn't understand?

She loved him. That thought she wrapped around her like a warm cloak. She walked home with a smile on her face, humming softly to herself.

Michael and Company

4

"Jeanie wasn't at school today."

Caroline, leaning against the stones of the churchyard wall, still warm from the day's sun, looked up under her lashes at Michael as he lounged on his favorite perch, languidly handsome, tossing that irresistible long blond lock out of his eyes. Since they had all been at primary school, it was the habitual perch of summer days, opposite the shop where they used to agonize over the spending of pocket money, then they'd reach the wall stickily laden with suckers and jawbreakers, chocolate bars or bubble gum.

But those days were long past. Caroline, tall, slim, sophisticated Caroline, would not have been seen dead with candy in her mouth.

Michael yawned. A student now—or at least, about to be—he couldn't be seen to be interested in the petty affairs of schoolgirls.

"Ill again, the little runt. Or was that poor mother of hers acting up?"

"She skipped school."

Caroline had his interest now. She basked, luxuriously, in the full force of those blue eyes she had suddenly realized, one day last spring, could make a delicious tingle run from her throat to the pit of her stomach.

"Never! She wouldn't have the nerve."

"How do you know, anyway? She might have been ill," Jim said from his place beside Michael on the wall, the place he had always occupied, even after the other boy left the village to go to boarding school and they met only at holidays.

Caroline ignored him and addressed herself pointedly to Michael.

"I saw her from the bus stop. She came out of her house with her school things, but when the bus came, she wasn't there."

Caroline looked triumphantly from one to the other of the boys. Impassively, they returned her gaze. Then they turned to each other and slowly shook their heads.

"Caroline," Jim said slowly and patiently, with his "dear old Caro—dense as two boards but we love her" expression on his face.

"Perhaps—she—missed—the—bus."

Caroline smiled, sweetly swinging her long blonde hair slowly back over one shoulder. This time she would have the last word.

"I saw her from the bus. I got on the top deck. She was standing behind the hedge in the field. She just stared at the bus until it went. She looked weird."

"Well, I always said she was crazy." Michael slid off the wall and stood brushing the dust from his jeans, dismissing his momentary interest in such petty things. He wandered nonchalantly over to the motorbike parked by

the bus stop, the one his Dad had bought him for passing
his exams, and straddled its black-and-chrome sleekness
with a swagger.

Jim, in his thoughtful way, was still pondering
Caroline's piece of information. He wasn't handsome like
Michael, she thought as she studied him, but at least he
didn't brush her off all the time. And he wasn't that
bad-looking. His face was sort of friendly, and funny,
especially when he screwed it up all sideways, as he was
now, running a hand through his rough brown hair.

"Robert Wylie won't speak to her," she offered,
making the best of the audience she had left. "You know
how they always used to have lunch together, thick as
thieves, and always talking away, goodness knows what
they found to talk about. She sits by herself now. And he
hangs around like a lost soul, just like he used to."

Michael, she could see out of the corner of her eye,
was apparently totally absorbed in making minute adjust-
ments to his rearview mirror. She turned her back on him
a little more firmly, and raised her voice so that he was
sure to hear.

"They weren't ever going out, though, were they?"
Jim asked. He was at Tech now, studying engineering.
Naturally easygoing, he couldn't emulate Michael's superior attitude to Caroline. After all, they'd all known each
other since they were toddlers.

"Well, not exactly. Though everyone could see it was
going that way. But now—I mean, can you imagine going
out with a girl who's liable to start foaming at the mouth
any minute? I don't blame him—nobody does. Anyway,
she's weird, always has been. I could never see what he

saw in her in the first place. She looks such a mess, that awful greasy hair of hers, and her clothes look as if they come from jumble sales. Do you remember that time in the third year she came to school with odd socks on? One gray and one blue? She said they were the only ones she could find! Can you believe it?"

It was the merest flicker in Jim's eyes that warned her to lower her voice. Too late, because Jeanie could already hear Caroline's shrill twitter before she turned the corner of the churchyard not ten yards away. She still remembered the incident of the socks with pain. It was not long after Dad died. Mom had been very bad for a week before, had hardly got out of bed. Jeanie had overslept, there was nothing in the house for breakfast and the laundry basket was overflowing on the bathroom floor. Hurrying to catch the bus, she hardly noticed the odd colors of the last two socks in the drawer until Caroline had been the first to point it out. The first of many.

Now Jeanie pushed down the rising flood of misery. She didn't want to spoil today. The warm calmness of loving Jake had carried her through her return home to her mother's blank face in front of the endlessly chattering television, the drawn curtains, last night's dishes in the kitchen sink. She had made a cup of tea and sat down beside her mother on the settee, reaching out a hand to her indifferent arm.

"It's a lovely day outside, Mom," she had said, wanting desperately to throw open the windows, to let in light and love. Mom said nothing, staring unseeing at the screen, sipping from her cup without turning her head. Jeanie might not have been there. There was no point in trying.

At least in the kitchen she could make her mark, she thought, when everything shone. In the garden she picked a bunch of Michaelmas daisies and arranged them in a jam jar on the windowsill.

She turned the corner and heard Caroline's voice die away, saw three pairs of eyes take her in. Jim looked away, embarrassed. She crossed the road quickly, head held high, and went into the shop. Outside she heard a motorbike engine roar into life.

"And how is your mother, dear?" Mrs. Palmer asked from behind the post office grille as she stamped the benefit book and counted notes on the counter. She asked this every week and never waited for a reply, going on without a break to the latest item of village gossip. She had an insatiable appetite for indignation. Today it was those hippie children she was convinced had been stealing from the candy display.

"And that young woman who's arrived now," the grating voice went on, "the one with the dark hair looking like it's never seen a comb, always wears men's clothes, something peculiar in that, I always say—anyway she was here last year, I remember her well. Bold as brass she is, had the nerve to come back with an apple she said had a maggot in it. And now here she is again, comes in with that misbegotten child of hers—no wedding ring, of course; oh no, not her sort, and the brat is a half-breed by the looks of it, but she's not ashamed of it. I don't know, I can't think how they get away with camping down there on the dunes. The Parish Council ought to do something about it."

Jeanie, ignoring her out of habit, was rummaging in

the freezer cabinet for something for tonight's meal. Beef-burgers, peas, french fries—that would do; she didn't feel like cooking. And they were out of dishwashing liquid. She added a loaf of bread to her basket and waited impatiently as Mrs. Palmer lumbered out from behind the post office grille and seated herself at the register, still talking. A wave of revulsion swept over Jeanie as she looked at the gray head bent over the keys. She was a gray person, Mrs. P. The words seemed to drip from her, a gray, stinking sludge that swilled around her ankles and crept across the floor. The stench was suffocating. Jeanie felt a cold sweat break out on her forehead. She had to get out.

"My mother's very depressed, if you must know," she found herself saying in a low, quick voice, snatching her change and pushing it into her pocket. "And I don't expect she'll ever get better. So I shouldn't bother to ask, if I were you."

She reached the doorway, shuddering and gasping for air, but not before she had seen Mrs. Palmer's mouth drop open with astonishment.

Outside the sunlight struck comfortingly warm on her goose-pimpling skin. Jim had slipped off the wall and was crossing the road. He passed her in the shop doorway.

"Don't mind those two," he muttered as he passed.

He was all right, Jim, when he got away from Michael's company.

Jeanie leaned on the wall until her brain cleared and the sick feeling passed. All of a sudden she couldn't help chuckling at the thought of Mrs. Palmer's shocked expression. That she, Jeanie, should speak to her like that!

Yesterday she would never have dared, would never even have thought of it. Was it deciding to skip school that had made the difference? Or falling in love? Or something to do with Jake himself? Whatever it was, she was no longer the Jeanie she used to be.

On the Beach Road

5

Across the road Caroline was arranging herself with the maximum display of long slender legs and a great deal of girlish giggling on the back of Michael's motorbike. He revved the engine violently, disturbing a cloud of pigeons who flew up with a clatter from the church roof. Then they were accelerating down the beach road in a cloud of dust, Caroline's shrieks drowning in the throaty roar of the bike and her arms clinging tight round the young man's waist, their heads defiantly unhelmeted.

Jeanie looked after them, glad they were gone, down the straight road to the distant gap in the dunes. Michael was going full speed on the empty road—empty, apart from three hazy figures, one large and two small, straggled out along the edge. One—the tall one—was leaning to gather something from the hedge, while the small ones darted in and out like a pair of small birds.

The bike was near them now. Traveling very fast, straight for the notch in the skyline. Straight for the two small figures half across the road. They froze, and Jeanie froze with them, unbelieving, terrified; as the black monster roared on, unswerving. Then she was running, hearing herself scream a warning, seeing the distant figure in the hedge straighten, leap, grab the little ones, and fall as the motorbike raced on towards the dune.

The reek of petrol filled her nostrils and she was gasping for breath. The bag of frozen food banged cold against her legs. She seemed to have been running for miles. She could see them still, huddled on the ground—a red-haired girl in a long turquoise skirt, a small boy with his arms wrapped around his head, and a little girl screaming in high-pitched terror, staring at a red trickle of blood running down her leg.

"Shush, Gwennie, that'll do; it's gone now, you're all right," the older girl was saying, pulling the child into her arms and rocking her.

She looked up as Jeanie came to a panting halt in front of them. She recognized the three now—the family from the hippie camp, the girl who had once helped her when her shopping bag broke outside the shop.

She crouched down, touching the shoulder of the boy, not knowing what to do, how to help.

"Are you all right?"

He shrank away as if her touch burnt him, turning on her a furious scowling face. Hurt, she took a step away.

"I'm sorry," was all she could say, feeling helpless tears rise in her throat. "I'm sorry."

A distant roar came from the direction of the sea. Jeanie whirled round.

"Look out!" she shrieked, frantically pulling at the little boy's arm, reaching out for the other two, hardly knowing what she was doing in the rising tide of panic, tugging at their weight until all four of them fell in a bruised tangle on the dusty grass of the bank at the edge of the road.

The bike had turned and was coming back towards them, faster than ever it seemed, a black bullet speeding out of the dunes, coming nearer, nearer. A wave of noise hit them, the hot wind buffeted their faces, the stench of exhaust rolled over them and with it a wild cry and the glimpse of two ecstatic faces, two fair heads, triumphant as pagan gods.

They were gone. Jeanie, sick and shaking, slowly raised her head from the ground where she had pressed herself as if to escape from her fear, wiping dry earth from her face.

The other girl put out a hand to touch hers, but didn't look at her. Freckles stood out starkly in a face blanched with fury as she stared up the road where the motorbike had already disappeared. A long breath hissed between her clenched teeth. Her rage alarmed Jeanie. She had been ready to like this girl, but her ferocity seemed too dangerous. She began to get to her feet. The movement brought Carla back to herself. She looked at Jeanie as if taking her in for the first time, and at once her face was transformed by a smile of delight. Impetuously she grasped Jeanie's hand and squeezed it hard.

"Thank you. I might have known it would be you."

Awkwardly, Jeanie turned to Gwennie, who was still clinging like a baby monkey to her sister. Stiff with terror, her arms and legs wound round Carla's body as far as they would go.

"Is she badly hurt?"

Carla unwound a hand from the back of her neck and looked tenderly into the child's face.

"It's OK now, lovely. They've gone. They won't come back. You can let go. You're bleeding on my skirt."

Laughing a little shakily, she gentled and comforted until Gwennie consented to unwind herself and have the cut on her leg attended to. Carla's voice, with its slight Welsh lilt, was as quiet and reassuring as the distant sound of the sea. Jeanie was content to watch and be calmed herself. Carla's mercurial change in mood, from fury to motherliness, fascinated her.

Carla mopped her sister's leg with a handkerchief, wiping away blood to reveal little more than a scratch. Slowly, Gwen's hysterical crying slowed to hiccuping sobs.

"He didn't hit her. She must have caught it on the brambles."

"Thank God for that. I'm so sorry."

"It's not your fault, you don't have to say sorry."

"I know, but I live here, I couldn't help feeling . . . Mrs. Palmer in the shop was saying horrible things . . . It all seemed like part of it."

Jeanie's legs gave way suddenly and she sat down by the roadside, leaning forward to pull uselessly at a spiky clump of grass. For a moment the anger flashed again in Carla's eyes, and her arms tightened round the child sitting on her lap.

"I know. I've seen it all my life. And now these two are having to learn. That's the worst of it." She bent her head to put her cheek against Gwen's hair, sighing enormously.

They had forgotten David, sitting hunched up to one side of them. When he leapt suddenly to his feet he startled them.

"He did it on purpose!" he yelled, his little face crimson with fury. "He's horrible! I hate him! Why did he do it, Carla? We haven't done anything to him!"

Together they looked at him silently, unable to make any reply. In that long moment Jeanie felt as if a bond was forged between them, a kind of sisterhood between strangers. In David's voice she heard Carla's, but also, echoing from far away, her own cry against what life had done to her, the protest she had never made. Did Carla feel this closeness too? Jeanie looked sideways at her, wanting her to, uncertain how to find out.

Carla stood up, brushing the dirt off her clothes with unnecessary vigor, as if to brush away what had happened.

"Come on, you two, we've got shopping to do." She set Gwen down on her feet, still clinging tightly to Carla's hand. David picked up a stone and flung it furiously down the road in the direction the bike had gone, then began walking as fast as he could ahead of them towards the village.

Carla turned to Jeanie. "Thanks for coming to help," she said shortly. "Not many would."

"I owe you one."

"You remember? I wasn't sure you'd even noticed me."

Suddenly Jeanie realized the meaning of Carla's earlier

remark. "I might have known it would be you." She had remembered—had even been waiting to meet her again.

"I noticed. But I'm better now." Jeanie stood straight, looked Carla directly in the eye, and almost laughed aloud.

"You must come and see us sometime, if you don't mind coming to the camp."

A challenge? With a kind of joy Jeanie saw that uncertainty was not all on her side. Carla, too, needed to be sure Jeanie accepted her.

"OK. I will."

"Tomorrow. I'll meet you on the beach if you like." Carla grinned mischievously. "Where you were this morning."

"This . . . Where?"

"I saw you. Dancing. In the sea."

Jeanie blushed and laughed with embarrassment. Carla was quick to reassure.

"Don't worry. You're not the only one to go a little mad sometimes. I was glad to see you happy. It was a beautiful morning. I'm not surprised you didn't want to go to school. Was it the beginning of the cure?"

"Maybe." Jeanie's guard came sharply up. She was not ready to say anything yet about Jake. She grinned cheerfully back, seeing with delight her own happiness reflected in Carla's face.

"OK. I'll be on the beach tomorrow evening. About seven."

Travelers

6

D ad, meet Jeanie."

She stood beside Carla in the middle of a rough circle of tents and vehicles tucked in behind the overshadowing dune which all but blocked out the constant murmur of the surf. In front of her a dense thicket of birch and alder sheltered the camp from view of the village; behind, a sandy track ran among dry turf and scrub towards the open fields. In the center of the circle, a neatly built brick fireplace released a thin trail of smoke and the lingering smell of roast meat. Beside it a lanky dog worried a bone, growled briefly at the stranger, and was hushed.

Carla's father clambered over the children playing on the steps of the bus and came to meet them with courteous hand outstretched. He was very tall, with shaggy dark hair and a luxuriant beard.

"I'm Chris. You're very welcome. Carla has told us all about you."

His educated voice was a surprise. He could have been a teacher, or even a man of property welcoming her to his domain. But Jeanie couldn't help staring at his threadbare corduroy trousers and overstretched jumper and, most of

41

all, at the grubby toes showing through holes in his canvas shoes. Aware of what an event her visit must be for them, she felt more shy and awkward than ever.

But Chris was all graciousness. With an odd little old-fashioned bow, he made a gesture which included the whole circle of makeshift dwellings.

"Make yourself at home. I'm afraid I'm in the middle of something, but Carla will show you round." Jeanie managed a small smile as she fidgeted from one foot to another, worrying that she might seem rude. Chris, unperturbed, gave Carla a little pat on the shoulder and walked away unhurriedly towards the far side of the camp.

"This is our bus."

It had been painted, a long time ago it seemed from the scattered pocks of rust, in a variety of gaudy colors, as if by someone clearing out old residues of paint. The window frames were yellow, the side panels blue and pink, the doors several shades of green, all of them faded by the sun into subtle variations. Each window had a different colored curtain—blue flowers, red and green stripes, purple swirls—so that the whole thing looked as if it had been brushed by a rainbow.

Carla was tugging at her hand, fizzing with pleasure and excitement. Jeanie got a grip on herself, trying to be a good guest, to make the right sounds of appreciation and interest.

"Come inside."

In the living space which took up about half the bus, Angharad, Carla's mother, sat curled up on a bunk beside the iron stove. Like Carla in coloring—red-haired and creamy-skinned—she was tiny and delicate, the small bones of her hand feeling birdlike even in Jeanie's grasp.

Jeanie took to her at once. She could see, looking around, Angharad's loving touches of detail that made the small space into a home—a painted vase full of wild honeysuckle, a lace mat, a cushion embroidered with flowers and butterflies. She waved them through to inspect the sleeping quarters, where Jeanie at last began to warm to her role, delighting Carla by exclaiming at the clever compactness of the bunks, the storage lockers and cupboards all built by Chris to house the family in surprising comfort.

"There's only one snag," Angharad's soft Welsh voice quivered with amusement. "He built it all so well that now the old bus is rotting away around them. We'll soon have our wonder-home with nothing to keep out the wet."

Mother and daughter rocked with laughter, leaving Jeanie at a loss. She could see it in her mind's eye—the bus in ruins and the family homeless.

"But what will you do? How much longer will it last?"

"Don't worry about us. We'll sort something out," Angharad said teasingly. "Who knows, we might even have to live in a house."

"Dad's always so thorough about everything," Carla explained. "Everything has to be perfect. It's a family joke."

Jeanie looked blank. Family jokes were something she didn't know about, or perhaps she had forgotten. Carla went on explaining.

"Then Dad teases Mom about being a Celtic princess.

It's sort of true—she's supposed to be descended from Llwelyn the Great—but he says it makes her full of dreams and totally impractical. We all laugh about it."

Flinging a friendly arm around Jeanie's shoulders, Carla led the way out and around to the back of the bus.

"Come and see the animals."

Chickens scratched around a wooden coop and wandered in and out of the low undergrowth. A tethered brown goat came expectantly towards them.

"Llwelyn was a great Welsh prince," Carla went on, noticing Jeanie's lost look. She scratched the goat behind its ears. "This is Tansy, by the way. I suppose they don't teach Welsh history in English schools. I've only ever been to school in Wales."

"You go to school, then?" Jeanie was glad to change the subject to something she understood.

"In the winter. We only travel in summer. Mom's brother has a place near Carmarthen where we always stay."

"You still live in the bus, though?"

"Oh yes. It's very cozy with the stove lit."

Tansy nuzzled Carla's pocket and she, laughing, produced an apple. Jeanie stood and watched, not reaching out to pat or stroke. She wasn't particularly fond of goats.

A little way away Owen squatted beside the woodpile, sharpening a knife on a stone. Carla called out to him, introducing Jeanie. Owen looked up and nodded without smiling.

"He's not unfriendly," Carla explained quietly. "It's

just that he can't be bothered with people very much. He's a loner, he likes to be off on his own with his dog."

That was a relief. At least it wasn't anything about her. Jeanie turned away, gesturing towards the rest of the encampment.

"Are these other people always with you?" she asked.

"No, no." Carla chuckled at the suggestion. "Come and see."

Two tents had been pitched directly across the circle from the bus. In the mouth of the first, an ancient khaki army tent, sat a girl not much older than they. Darkly shadowed eyes looked out from a face so pale and gaunt that Jeanie wondered if she had been dreadfully ill. As they came up to her she realized with disgust that her skin was gray with ingrained dirt. She appeared to be wearing nothing but an oversized man's shirt. Jeanie felt as if she was looking at one of those pictures of Third World poverty from a charity advertisement. Carla, still cheerful, seemed not to have noticed.

"Hi, Terry."

The girl smiled nervously and turned away to speak to someone inside the tent. A round-faced boy with short-cropped hair pushed aside the hanging tent flap and grinned up at them from where he lay on a pile of greasy sleeping bags.

"Hi, Carla, this your friend? I'm Sean."

Sean was ready enough to talk. They were from Birmingham and had been here a month. They weren't travelers really, just "needed somewhere to go." It was good here, quiet, and out of the way. Chris had been kind to them, helped them out one way and another.

As he talked Sean pulled at a silver earring and scratched his chest under a grubby vest, while Terry watched him, her eyes hungrily devouring his face. Jeanie's mind filled with alarming questions. If they weren't here, would they be on the streets in a cardboard box? Had they run away? From their families? The police? She didn't like the possibilities she saw. She didn't know how Carla's family could let them stay. She didn't want to know. She tugged at Carla's sleeve.

"Who else is there?"

Carla moved on reluctantly, not understanding Jeanie's unease. The other tent was different, bright green and newish. A football pennant saying *Sunderland* fluttered from the guy-rope.

Gary and Phil weren't travelers either, they said. Two stocky lads from up North, almost indistinguishable in faded denims, they were only there for the summer. Apart from that they said little, watching Jeanie suspiciously as if she might give them away to someone she knew nothing of. Was there more in their presence than they admitted? She pulled herself up. *Prejudice,* she told herself, just like the village. *You don't know.*

"No point hangin' round waiting for work when there isn't none," Phil said shortly, turning back to the motor-bike parts spread out on the grass.

"Got to get it back together or we'll never get home!" Gary explained cheerfully.

Their tent smelled of stale socks and beer. It was almost as if they were there on holiday.

So half of them weren't hippies at all. To Carla, the distinction didn't seem to have any meaning. Now they crossed the camp towards the only other vehicle, a battered blue van backed in between two trees.

Without having seen her before, Jeanie recognized the occupant. She sat on the back step with her knees drawn up, watching their progress curiously and waiting for them to come her way. The dungarees, the wild hair, the baby clothes hung to dry on the bushes made her unmistakable. This was the dreadful woman who had so much alarmed Mrs. Palmer in the shop. Already Jeanie was ready to like her.

Her name was Jo. Her eyes, bright and small like a shy animal's, watched Jeanie as if from under cover. Although ready enough to talk, she was nervous and guarded. Only when she picked up the baby from his nest inside the van did her brittleness melt.

"He's called Pippin, and he's five months old."

Pippin looked straight at Jeanie with his round black eyes and smiled toothlessly, the satiny skin of his cheeks dimpling perfectly. Hardly knowing what she was doing, Jeanie held out her arms for him and the next moment was holding a baby, as she had never done before. The wave of tenderness took her breath away.

"He's lovely."

Jo smiled back proudly, a warmth surfacing at last. Somehow Jeanie knew that something of the same feeling had once taken her by surprise, too.

They'd known Jo for years, Carla explained as they

walked away. They camped together on and off. But recently she'd been different, since she'd been in the Battle of the Beanfield. "The what?" Jeanie was about to ask, but Carla was explaining already. A lot of travelers had gathered at Stonehenge one year. The police, ordered to disperse them, had attacked them brutally where they were camped in a field. Jo had her van windows broken, her face cut, and spent the night in a cell. She never trusted outsiders now. Even her friends found her a bit unsociable. And now that she had Pippin she could be fierce—like a lioness with one cub.

"It's a good thing you took to him or she'd have nothing to do with you."

The story of the Beanfield rang vague bells in Jeanie's head. Something she had heard on the TV news, perhaps. Only not the way Carla told it.

Angharad put her head out of the window, asking them to shut up the hens. Carla took a scoop of corn from a metal bin and scattered a few grains, watching the hens come clucking eagerly to her feet. Together the girls counted them into the coop, filled up their water trough and left them for the night.

Jeanie's head was full of thoughts, questions she did not like to ask. Most of the things people said about the hippies weren't true. They weren't dirty—those that were weren't real travelers—and the camp wasn't a slum. On the whole it was tidy and organized. But here were lots of things she didn't understand. Why didn't they live like other people? Such an odd assortment—all held together by a kind of not belonging, but for such different reasons. And what did they live on? Eggs, milk, fish—there had to be more. Perhaps it was true that they sponged off the state—though they didn't seem to need very much.

It was such an insecure way to live, in an old bus that could fall apart any minute. No thought for the future, only a day at a time. She didn't know if she could cope with that. Though again, look at her and Mom. Dependent on the state. What if Mom's health failed altogether? She preferred not to think about that.

At least Carla's family had each other—squabbles, no doubt, like all families, but laughter too, and everyone seemed to help out. She had the feeling the whole group would stick together in a crisis, which was more than could be said for Sea Norton with its gossip and petty feuds.

The best thing was feeling welcome. They were far more at ease with her than she was with them. She looked round for Carla, realizing she had been standing for some time staring vaguely at the trees. She wanted her to know she was glad to be here.

"Thank you for asking me. I've enjoyed meeting everyone."

Carla was so pleased she almost hugged her.

"You can come any time you like. You're almost one of us now."

Carla meant every word, but all the same Jeanie knew it wasn't true. It was rather disturbing to find that the thought made her shrink, ever so slightly, away from her friend.

A Spy in the Camp

7

Angharad had stirred the fire to life and hung a blackened kettle from the big pothook. The girls perched on thick logs of smooth driftwood, grateful for the warmth of the flames on their bare legs as the evening air cooled. Gwen came and leaned against Carla, sucking her thumb. As the kettle's song gradually settled to a boil, the travelers gathered one by one at the camp's focal point according to their different natures. Jo sat upright, cross-legged on the ground, with Pippin asleep on her lap. Phil and Gary lounged in old car seats, sharing a can of beer. Sean and Terry huddled close together, a little apart from the rest, a gray blanket wrapped around their shoulders. In the center Chris squatted, leaning over the fire to catch its light as he carefully took apart a door latch, laying screws and small metal parts out on a cloth so as not to lose them.

Talk passed to and fro along with the mugs of tea, an idle chewing over of the day. As dusk fell the small circle of firelight became an enclosure, the circle of faces in the flickering glow all that there was to see. Jeanie watched without hearing until the current of conversation eddied around her and caught her in its flow, and suddenly she was the center of attention.

"Do you know the young man who attacked Carla and the children yesterday?" asked Chris, settling his hot mug of tea carefully on a level patch of ground. He looked up at her sharply under his dark, bushy eyebrows, shrewd and attentive. He made Jeanie nervous, as if she were a witness in court.

"Yes—no—not very well. I mean, I used to—he's always been round, but he was away at school. His name's Michael Richardson, and he's the doctor's son."

Suddenly she felt like a traitor. She had to say something in Michael's defense.

"He didn't attack them. Gwen was frightened and fell into the brambles."

"It was still an attack. Even if no one had been hurt at all, the intention was to intimidate by superior force. Technically I believe one could make a case for assault."

Chris's deep voice had the caress of steel, and his eyes seemed to accuse. Did he think the whole world was against him? And was she part of that world? Yet they had welcomed her. It was confusing. She didn't want to defend Michael. He had always been hateful to her.

"Take it easy, Chris. It's all right, Jeanie, don't let him get to you."

Angharad was leaning forward, laying a restraining hand on her husband's arm.

"He trained as a barrister. He forgets people aren't used to being cross-examined."

"I'm sorry," Chris wiped a hand across his face as if to

brush away the past. "It would help us, though, if you could tell us a little about the boy. Then we'd know if we really need to worry."

This was better. Carefully, without emotion, Jeanie began with the facts.

"I've known Michael since I was little. He's eighteen, three years older than me, and we both went to the village school. I didn't like him. He used to bully everyone. Then he went to boarding school. He left in July. He's supposed to go to college next month. His parents bought him the bike, and he's mad about it. He's done nothing but roar about and show off on it ever since. Everyone complains about the noise, but no one will say anything to Dr. Richardson. All the old women think Michael's a wonder-boy anyway."

Jo's fierce eyes flashed.

"Showing off, is it? If that's what he does when he's showing off, what happens when he really wants to do damage?"

Her arms tightened protectively around her baby, who half-woke with a little protesting cry.

Again Jeanie couldn't help feeling it was she who was under attack. She tried to think clearly. Could Michael deliberately hurt for pleasure? Yes, came the answer, sickeningly sure. She knew he could. But a part of her still could not betray someone who she had grown up with. These people had welcomed her, but how would they use what she told them?

"I—I don't think he does want to do damage. The

girl, Caroline, she eggs him on. He was trying to be macho, I think."

Suddenly she saw again the naked blood-lust on Michael's face as he had roared off up the beach road, and she shuddered and fell silent. The assembled company waited. Wretchedly, Jeanie tried to give them the answer they wanted, but the more she struggled, the less she seemed able to say.

"I don't really know. He's grown up now. I only knew him when I was little. Maybe he's changed."

She remembered the thoughtless arrogance with which he had constantly wounded her as a child. She had never even dared hate him for it, just instinctively kept out of his way, as the runt of the litter avoids the boss puppy. Only now he wasn't a puppy anymore—with his bike and his male strength he was beginning to be dangerous.

From the intent faces around her she thought they understood not only what she had said, but also her silence and her reasons for it. A separation had grown between her and the travelers. She belonged with her people, they with theirs. But also, she realized wonderingly, they respected her loyalties.

"Well?" With a gesture Chris laid the subject open for discussion.

"Carla?"

"That boy hates us. We're scum to him. I've seen it in his face. Most people here look down on us, but with him it's something worse. I think he'd really hurt us if he could."

For the first time Jeanie heard Owen speak, with a slight hesitation in his voice that was not quite a stammer.

"There's a group of bikers who ride in the dunes farther up the coast. One of them looks like this Michael. The rest are older, tough-looking. I wouldn't want to get involved with them."

Chris, frowning, turned to Jeanie with eyebrows raised. She shrugged.

"I don't know. If Michael were hanging about people his parents wouldn't approve of, he'd stay clear of the village. But the way he's mad about that bike, it wouldn't surprise me."

She fell more easily, now, into her witness role, understanding what they wanted of her, happy to please. Just so long as this was not the only reason Carla had asked her to come. With a painful stab of doubt she looked at the girl beside her. Carla's face was taut with concentration as the discussion moved towards decision. Should they move on before trouble came? Stay on and hope for the best? Or, as Gary suggested, teach Michael a lesson before worse happened?

"I could think of a few things to do to his precious bike if I knew where he kept it."

Jeanie sat silent, forgotten as the debate went back and forth. Into her empty mind wormed a familiar train of thought. Carla hadn't really wanted to be friends. The warmth, the smiles, were not really for her. It was all wishful thinking. Overcome by a sudden flood of misery, she was on the point of trying to slip away from the firelight before anyone noticed her.

"Listen!" Owen held up his hand. Beneath Owen's other hand, his dog's ears pricked up, listening to the wind. As the talk died away the lurcher's body trembled and a low growl rumbled in his chest. In the silence they all heard the whine of motorbikes, suddenly becoming a roar as they turned the corner of the track beyond the trees.

"Into the bus! Quick!"

Carla and her mother were on their feet, shooing the children in front of them. Jo gathered up Pippin and ran. The rest scattered. In a moment the camp was deserted. Only Jeanie failed to react. She sat on beside the fire, shocked, unable to pull herself from the dark well of thoughts into which she felt herself falling. She heard the grinding crescendo of the engines, but could not take her eyes from a spreading pool of tea from an overturned mug slowly seeping into the ground. Branches crashed, the roar faltered, then came on, deafening. She put her hands over her ears.

"Jeanie!" she heard Carla scream from the bus door.

She looked up, seeing the red hair, the white face, the open mouth, the terror. At the edge of her vision the first black-helmeted rider thrust through the bushes and came straight towards her. She rolled off her seat, wrapped her head in her arms and lay still, her knees pulled up and her face pressed to the dry, sandy turf.

A deafening roar, a hot stench, the wind of their passing. She pressed herself hard to the log she had been sitting on, trying to be invisible. The ground shook. One, two, three, four bikes rampaged through the camp, swerved around and were gone, crashing through undergrowth back to the track and away into the distance. A cacophony of dogs barking, terrified chickens cackling, then, at last, silence. Jeanie slowly uncurled and lay still with her eyes closed, listening to the dim roar of the sea beyond the dune. They were not coming back.

A hand touched her shoulder. Carla. Jeanie pushed herself up to a sitting position. She was shaking.

"Are you all right?"

Jeanie nodded. "Is everybody else?"

She looked round. Chris was emerging from the bus. From behind it came Owen, tugging the goat by a rope attached to its collar.

"Tansy pulled out her stake," he reported laconically, and turned back again into the darkness. A moment later there was the rhythmic clang of hammer against steel.

From the direction of Jo's van came Sean, his arms around Terry, who looked younger and paler than ever and shook with sobs. Angharad went over to them and took Terry's arm kindly.

"You'd better come in with us tonight. You never know if they'll be back."

Terry clung to Angharad, her crying rising to a wail like a little girl's. The older woman soothed her, guiding her towards the bus. Sean, dazed, followed obediently behind.

The two boys collected their mugs and burrowed into their tent, talking in an undertone. Chris checked the dogs' chains and began to bank up the fire, making normality return while the shockwaves still trembled in the air. They were strong, Jeanie thought. They will survive.

"I'd better go. Thanks again for inviting me. I'm glad I've met you people."

"You'll be all right?"

"Of course I will."

Another thought hung between them, unspoken, creating a separating chasm. Jeanie was in no danger. Not from her own people. If those were her people. Jeanie knew with an almost physical sickness that she wanted nothing to do with them.

Impulsively she reached out for Carla's hand. Carla pulled Jeanie towards her and hugged her, quick and strong. It was so long since anyone had put their arms around her that it brought a lump to Jeanie's throat. With a mumbled good-bye she pulled away and walked off into the rapidly gathering darkness. Whatever she was to Carla, she thought, for the others she was still just a spy in the other camp.

Footsteps behind her made her spine prickle. A voice called her name. She stopped and waited until a shadow turned into the stocky form of one of the Sunderland lads. Phil, she decided, the shorter one.

"Jeanie! Wait a minute!"

He came up to her at a brisk, silent trot on his bare feet, then he swore as he stepped on something sharp and hopped around so that she couldn't help laughing.

"Never mind that," Phil stood on one leg and went on impatiently. "I wanted to ask you something. This Michael—where does he live?"

"In the old vicarage—down the little lane beside the churchyard."

"Thanks."

He turned away abruptly and limped off the way he had come.

That was it, she thought. She was just a useful informer. A tremor in her mind worried that she had given away something she shouldn't, but she suppressed it. Gary and Phil were not like Michael. And if she hadn't told them, they would have found out some other way.

What Would You Do?

8

On Saturday a white wall of sea mist rolled in over the dunes. Only a mile or two inland the sun was shining, but the village and the flat fields of the coastland were dank and chilly. Jeanie pushed aside branches wet with hanging droplets as she approached Jake's hut through the orchard, but could not brush aside the turmoil of her feelings.

So much had happened in the two days since she met Jake. When she thought about it, she was sure it was all due to him. Without him, she never would have had the energy to go to Carla's aid, let alone respond to her invitation to the camp. Until the day before yesterday it had taken all her strength just to keep going, one day at a time.

Nor would yesterday have happened. She still didn't know how she could have done it. Instead of mumbling something to her tutor about being ill (it was easy—she was ill often enough), she had been amazed to hear herself telling the truth.

"I couldn't face school yesterday," she had said. "Things got too much for me."

She had known Mrs. Leader was a kind person. At the

beginning of term she had called Jeanie over and told her to come to her if she had troubles. Without referring to anything in front of the rest of the class, she had made it clear that she understood.

Jeanie, hating to be singled out, had looked away, shuffled her feet, and escaped. Now Mrs. Leader almost leapt to respond to Jeanie's unexpected admission. She actually seemed pleased to be allowed to help. She would see that the persecution in school was dealt with. Perhaps the school nurse could come and talk to the class about epilepsy. She even offered to find out about help at home, promising that there was no question of separation from Mom. At a stroke, a window of hope had opened. All in the space of two days.

But it was Jake who had really made things different. She still puzzled over how it had come about. All he had done was listen to her. Again and again she asked herself what it was about him that drew her to him so strongly. Like her, he was a loner, an outsider, different. But he was content with it. He liked being himself, and that enabled him to like and accept Jeanie as herself. Was that all it was?

Her feelings told her a different story. Alone, she had thought of him almost continuously; when she was not thinking of him she was still aware of him, as if everything she did was somehow important to him as well as to herself. She felt as if he was standing beside her all the time, reassuring, helping, strengthening.

Of course he was not, her rational self said scornfully. He did not know what she was doing, he had probably forgotten about her. It was as if there were two Jakes, the real one and the one in her mind. In her imagination, Jake wrapped around her with love, in her dreams he held her safe in his arms. But the real Jake . . . She almost couldn't bear to go to him in case he was altogether different and didn't care about her at all—in case it had all been fantasy.

She had made him a blackberry pie. Her hands were sticky from clutching it too tightly. It was her insurance policy. At least if he didn't want her, she could just say she had come to say thank you, leave her gift, and go away again.

The door was shut. She knocked and waited. Nothing happened. She stood on the doorstep looking dully around at the ghostly trees. Should she leave the pie and go home?

She had to try to look inside. As she nervously turned the handle, she half expected for a wild moment to find the hut full of farm junk, as it had been years ago, and Jake a figment of her imagination. But there was the bright blanket, the table with the stove, the orderly sparseness of Jake's belongings, just as it had been—thank God. She leaned on the door, weak with relief. He had been there, he was there. He could not be far away.

She set the pie down on the table and hovered uncertainly beside it, wondering whether to sit and wait. Then the noise started.

A rhythmic noise, thrum, thrum, rapid and short. Then in counterpoint, a harsh grinding. Silence. Then again. She could feel a throbbing in her feet through the wooden floor. She reached out a hand to touch the back wall, and felt it hum against her fingertips. Inside, but beyond the wall? She realized suddenly how much bigger the building looked from the outside. Another room, but not accessible from this one. Another way in.

She was running a well-trodden pathway around the side of the building. Another window, curtained with festoons of dusty cobwebs. An open door.

"Jake!"

She hung on to the doorpost to stop herself from running into his arms. Happiness welled up and burst painfully inside her. Weak and breathless, she continued to hang on, too overwhelmed to move.

He looked up, took in her radiant face, her adoring eyes, and smiled at her gently, affectionately, like an older brother.

"Hello, Jeanie. I thought you would be back."

Slowly her joy faded, cooled, ran away from her. Jake knew what she felt, and without words he said no to the dangerous passion of her imagination. It hurt. He didn't want her love. But he was still looking at her with that open, generous smile of his. Could there be another kind of love that she could share with him? Encouraging, accepting, unconditional? Not belonging to him, not putting herself under his feet in adoration, but being with him and being herself?

For a moment she seemed to see Jake's way spread out before her in all its beauty. Yet letting go of her dream hurt too much. She could not do it, not yet. Perhaps one day she would. She came slowly to his side, feeling her way to understanding, knowing herself a little more with every step.

Then as she took in the odd contraption in front of her which must be the source of that particular noise, curiosity and astonishment drove deep feelings completely out of her mind.

"What are you doing?"

Jake sat facing a wooden trestle. On the other side of it, two posts driven into the earth floor supported a long, springy pole, one end to the ground, the other curving high over his head. Tied to the end of the pole was a cord which came vertically down to a roughly rounded piece of wood fixed on the trestle between two brackets. The cord wound around the wood, then went to a triangular treadle hinged to pegs in the floor. The piece of wood turned slowly, then faster as he began to pedal rhythmi-cally—thrum, thrum—thrum, thrum.

"Whatever is it?" The whole gadget looked so much like a joke machine she had trouble keeping herself from giggling.

He chuckled, delighted at her perplexity. She began to feel at ease with him again.

"It's a pole lathe. I know it looks as if it's put together with string—it is, really. But it does work. Watch."

Maintaining the rhythmic tread of his foot on the pedal, he picked up a sharp tool from the bench beside him and, steadying it on the back of the other hand, gently brought it to bear on the whirling wood. A long rasp with each turn, and shavings began to trickle to the floor. Slowly, the wood melted away, corners rounded, a shape began to appear. He changed tools, making grooves and ridges. Then the machine stopped and Jake was detaching a banister rod to put into Jeanie's hands. She turned it over, feeling its slight roughness, amazed that something so finished could come from this contraption of nails and string.

"It's good."

She could see he took pleasure in her praise. She was glad to be able to give something back to him. He took the rod again and began smoothing it with a piece of sandpaper, handling the wood lovingly with sensitive fingers, stroking the grain as its texture began to appear.

"My grandfather made a living turning chair legs with a lathe like this. He showed me how to use it when I was a kid. I like to do it this way. It's simple, and it works."

Mentally, Jeanie checked off another question she had wanted answered. He had to have some way of earning a living. She liked the way his life seemed all of a piece, and that this fitted with everything else she knew about him. Simple, he had said. Like the rest of him—his needs, his home, the way he took people as they were.

"And people want to buy what you make?" she asked.

"Ah," Jake grinned cheerfully. "Lots of people are fixing up old cottages around here, replacing the things the woodworm ate. I can do it cheap—and they like to think it's been done the same way the old one was."

"And you can actually live like this—so . . . so . . ." She tried again. "You don't worry about having enough, and rainy days, and things like that?"

"See how the lilies of the field grow," Jake said softly. "They do not labor or spin. Yet I tell you that not even Solomon in all his splendor was dressed like one of these . . ."

For a moment she was not sure if he was serious. But

he was, looking at her in that straight way he had as if he was trying to tell her something and she didn't understand the code. She had to turn away, pick up a tool from the bench, put it down again, and walk to the door. It gave her a prickly feeling that she didn't know how to cope with.

But when she turned back he was smiling in the old way. He stood up briskly, brushing the sawdust from his clothes.

"Time for a cup of tea."

The blackberry pie, forgotten, lay on the table in a pool of its oozing juice. His boyish delight at the gift made her laugh and forget her unease. The kettle chuckled on the stove and the hut became warm and cozy. Jeanie never heard the swishing footsteps in the long grass. It was the creak of the door that made her look up and almost choke on a hot mouthful of tea as Carla's flaming head pushed through the opening.

"Carla! Come in! You're just in time for the last piece of pie. Jeanie—this is Carla. Carla . . ."

The two girls were staring at each other open-mouthed.

"Don't tell me you've met already?" Jake was shaking his head as if in amusement at some private joke. "So it's all arranged. I was going to introduce you."

In a moment they were both pouring out the story of their meeting, of Michael and the incident on the beach road, and finally of the motorcyclists' assault on the travelers' encampment.

"They haven't been back again?" Jeanie asked anxiously.

"No. But we've heard them, circling in the dunes, reminding us that they're there. Everyone's very worried. Dad and Mom say we mustn't give in to them, and we won't go unless things get really nasty. But I don't like it. I don't feel free any more. We only have to offend them in some way we don't even know about, and they could really hurt us."

Carla looked at Jake then. She had come to him, Jeanie saw at once, because Carla trusted him just as Jeanie did. A momentary pang of fierce jealousy shot through Jeanie, but with a great effort she refused it room. She needed both of them too much.

Carla brought her clenched fist down on the table. Emotion all but strangled her voice.

"It's horrible being like this. There must be something we can do. I can't just sit and let it happen, this violence, this fear—it's wrong, it's evil, and I hate it. But what can you do against people like that? I wanted to ask you, Jake, what would you do?"

Peacemaker

9

As the two girls walked home together by the track that followed the back of the dunes, Carla told Jeanie how she had come across the hut in the orchard while looking for half-wild plums.

"He's an odd one," she said, picking a tall stem of yellowing grass from beside the path and stripping the hairy seeds bit by bit. "He moves around, but he's not really a traveler. He doesn't know how he could exist on his own like that."

"He's not like anyone else," Jeanie agreed happily. She had taken off her shoes and the sand beneath her feet was pleasurably warm in the hazy sunshine. A mild breeze had blown away the mist and now gently lifted the hair from her neck and caressed her bare arms. The sharp tang of sea air tickled her nostrils. She felt it all intensely, full of a warm contentment that came from the morning spent with Jake. She loved him. Yes, she understood the rules that, without a word, he had laid down. Yes, she accepted them because he had made them. But the way she felt had not changed, and the best thing in the world was being close to him.

"He has a way of talking that makes you feel he knows

what's right," Carla was saying. "Not like most people, who say well, if this, then that, and you could see it this way, but on the other hand . . . That's why I wanted to talk to him. No one else has any answers. And he understands why I get angry about the way things are. Not like Dad, who's always being reasonable, or Mom, who keeps saying it'll all turn out for the best, when you know it won't. When I listen to Jake, I believe him, but then it doesn't seem real. How can you just do something because it's right, when you don't know whether people will see it too, especially when they could take advantage of you?"

With an effort Jeanie brought her mind back from its wordless song of happiness.

"Don't give back evil for evil," Jake had said when they told him about Michael and the bikers. "Give love instead of hate; say things that will heal, not hurt."

It frightened her, the thought of giving love to people who despised and tormented her. It wasn't just Michael, it was practically everyone. How could she love them? Avoidance was the best she could do, keeping the peace, hoping not to provoke. Giving love meant making it even easier for them to hurt you. She didn't think it was possible for her. For Jake, perhaps—but he was so strong, so sure of himself.

"I mean, what would actually happen if we tried to make peace with the bikers, did something nice for them, invited them to tea?" Carla went on, arguing with herself, hardly aware of Jeanie. "Do you really think they'd suddenly turn around and like us? They'd probably just despise us as wimps, realize we weren't going to defend ourselves, and things would be worse than before."

She subsided into silence, tugging at the grass again but this time angrily, scattering seeds and shredded stems in the tall undergrowth.

Jeanie didn't reply. Just for a moment she saw it, what Jake had meant. It wasn't that you had to be strong. More a matter of accepting you might fail, but doing it anyway. Because it was good, it was a blow struck on the right side. The germ of an idea was growing inside her. Could she . . . ? What could they do, after all, that they hadn't already done?

Both girls were still silent and preoccupied as they parted at the alder trees that screened the camp. Jeanie, her mind made up, set off purposefully towards the village.

Thick, dark trees cloaked the little lane that ran beside the churchyard to the old parsonage, a rambling red brick house, half-covered in Virginia creeper. When the village and its church had flourished, the vicar of the parish had lived here, doubtless with his large, Victorian family. You could imagine him with side-whiskers, driving up in a pony and trap, or clean-faced little girls in pinafores playing in the shrubbery that grew thick against the churchyard wall.

Jeanie walked calmly between the brick pillars of the gateway and crunched along the gravel of the drive, remembering the day, so many years ago now, when she had come here in her best clothes to one of Michael's lavish birthday parties, to which every child in the village was invited. To her relief, he had ignored her. His mother had been kind, in a brusque kind of way.

It was Mrs. Richardson who answered the door—tall, gray-haired and healthily tanned, dusting earth from faded brown trousers and a man's shirt without a collar.

"I'm sorry, I was in the garden . . . Oh, Jeanie!" She stopped, for once without words. She, too, remembered the shadowy child, face always turned half away, who had so oddly touched her that long-ago day. Now here she was on her doorstep, looking directly at her with unfamiliar, striking eyes.

"Hello, Mrs. Richardson. Is Michael at home?" Jeanie asked quickly, before she lost her nerve.

"Yes, I think so. I—I'll just go and see."

She turned and went back into the house, in her amazement absentmindedly abandoning Jeanie on the doorstep. She waited, hearing footsteps on the stairs, an increasingly exasperated voice calling Michael's name. Then a faint, deep-voiced reply. A door opened.

"I had my headphones on. I didn't hear," said in pacifying, injured tones.

Footsteps padded down the stairs. There was Michael, golden and immaculate in jeans and clean white shirt, hands on hips, staring down at her.

To her astonishment, now that she was here, she had no impulse to run away.

"Well?"

His tone was contemptuous, his whole lithe, tanned body expressing ineffable scorn. Yet Jeanie sensed his uncertainty. She had surprised him, and he was no longer sure she was the girl he had always taken her to be. She was not afraid of him.

"I want to talk to you about the travelers."

His mouth was already twisting into a sneer, but the beauty of those huge gray eyes looking up at him so trustingly suddenly caught him and momentarily held back his anger. Jeanie went on hurriedly, knowing instinctively that she did not have long.

"They're just ordinary people, really. I've talked to them. They want to be left in peace. The children were very frightened the other day. They haven't done anything to hurt you. Please, leave them alone!"

"I'll do what I like." Michael's voice was little more than a whisper. He glanced over his shoulder, not wanting to be overheard. He wanted to get rid of her, this girl who dared come to his home, risking his parents' putting their noses in where they were not wanted. He already had the door half-closed.

"Now go away, Jeanie, stay at home with your mother, and mind your own business. OK?"

The door banged shut in her face, and he was gone. Shaken by her failure, Jeanie stood on the doorstep, staring at the brass knocker just inches from her eyes. Carla had been right. It didn't do any good. She began to hurry down the drive, head down in her old way, already blaming herself for even thinking that anything she could do would be of any use.

"Jeanie?"

She had not seen Dr. Richardson coming in at the gate from a local call, black bag in hand. She looked up sharply to see his pleasant, lined face looking at her with a worried frown.

"Is everything all right? Were you looking for me?"

"Yes, thank you, I mean no, I . . ." she faltered, wondering for a blinding moment if she should tell him everything. But it would be no use. How could he believe her word against that of his son: wonderful, clever, handsome Michael, the apple of his father's eye?

"Is your mother OK? I'll come and take a look at her next week, it's a while since I last called." The doctor made an attempt at an encouraging smile, but was clearly still puzzling over what Jeanie was doing in his driveway. Jeanie didn't try to explain. She simply walked away past him, out of the gates and down the lane. The doctor stared after her, sighed and shook his head, then slowly turned away and went into the house.

Jeanie walked blindly on, heading for home without thinking. You've probably made things worse, went the relentless voice in her head. Whatever could make you think Michael would listen to you? You! He's right to despise you, you've never done anything worthwhile, you're stupid, crazy, useless. Trying to do things the way Jake does them! That's a joke! What makes you think you could do, or be, anything remotely like him?

Stop it! Jeanie's inner scream almost burst out of her. It was the thought of Jake that made her rebel against the voice in her head, the one she had listened to most of her life. *Jake doesn't see me like this*, she said to herself. *He thinks I'm a worthwhile person, and if he thinks it, it must be true.*

She had stopped in her tracks and was standing beside the side gate leading into the churchyard. It was cool and quiet in there. She slipped in and sat down with her back against a tree, breathing deeply to calm herself. She'd work herself into a fit if she went on like this. Better now. She felt quietness and confidence come back, began to feel her new self returning. It was crazy to let Michael get to her like that. He was only a boy a little older than herself, after all. She remembered him when they had been at the village school together, already lording it over the smaller boys, always with his little gang of followers and his faithful lieutenant at his side.

That was it! Jim! Jim Benton! He would listen to her. He had always been the one who had a word to say to her, even sometimes apologizing about Michael like the other day. She would go and see Jim. If anyone could get Michael to listen, he could.

Don't give up, Jeanie, she told herself. *There must be a way.*

Jim was in the back garden of his parents' cottage, tinkering with his bike. Michael's parents had bought him a powerful new motorbike, but it was as much as the Bentons could manage to get Jim a decent cycle to ride to college on. Jim's dad was a fisherman and in charge of the inshore lifeboat. Everybody in the village respected him. Jim took after him, trustworthy and sensible, except in one thing.

Surprised, Jim smiled uncertainly as he scrambled to his feet, wiping his hands on a rag. He listened attentively, frowning when Jeanie came to the bit about Michael and his biking companions' sortie into the traveler camp.

"I knew he was hanging about with some bikers from the town," he said when she had finished. "To be honest, I haven't seen a lot of him lately, not since he got the bike. One of that gang—Skull, he's called, they all have funny names—must be at least thirty-five. They're all older than Mike, and I don't like what I've seen of them. Mike's changed. He takes too much notice of them. He wouldn't have done a thing like that otherwise—you know him, Jeanie. He's not really bad."

Jim looked appealingly at Jeanie, who couldn't help being reminded of a dog caught in disobedience. He was so loyal, so devoted, and now his oldest friend had deserted him. She wanted to comfort him, but recalling the terror in Gwennie's face, she made herself be firm.

"You saw him the other day on the beach road. He wasn't with them then. Somebody's got to stop him. I've tried, and he won't listen to me. But he might listen to you. It's for his sake too, you know that. He'll get into trouble if things go on. Please—try and talk to him."

Jim sighed deeply and turned away from her, picked up a fallen wrench, and twisted it in his hands.

"I don't know, Jeanie. I've always been the one who's done what he says. I don't think he'll listen to me."

"But you can try. It won't hurt if you fail—at least you'll have done your best. I tried, and it was harder for me."

He looked at her then with dawning respect, seeing for the first time with wonder how hard it must have been for her to walk up to Michael's front door.

"OK, Jeanie. I'll try."

He held out his hand and she shook it. She felt elated. She had done it. Jim had listened to her. She, Jeanie Grant, was beginning to make things happen. *Thank you,* she said to the Jake in her head.

Night Prowlers

10

Carla, I'm frightened."

Carla turned sleepily in her bunk, reaching out a hand to the small nightgowned figure she could just make out standing beside her.

"It's all right, Gwennie. Did you have a bad dream?"

"Can't sleep. I keep thinking about the men."

Carla shifted across the bed to make room for her little sister, wrapping her arms and feet around the small shivery body, and burying her face in the silky hair. With a sudden squeeze, she growled in Gwen's ear so that she giggled and shrieked.

"There. You're safe with me. Carla won't let them get you. I'll jump out and frighten them off like a big brown bear."

Gwennie snuggled down into the warmth of her sister's bed. She and Carla had their own special jokes together. Carla had adored her ever since she had arrived, a baby made easily frightened, but always ready to respond with delight to a friendly face. Growing up, Gwen glowed and thrived on her sister's devotion, confident so long as she could come back for safety and a big hug.

For days now, Carla had watched sadly as Gwen became uncertain and withdrawn, sitting in the corner of the bus, sucking her thumb instead of going out to play with David. The bikers haunted her. At the sound of a tractor engine in a distant field she would stiffen and freeze, wide-eyed. When the bikers began their cruel teasing, passing back and forth on the track and in the dunes, Carla had to hold her, white and shaking, until they had gone. At night she woke whimpering from dreams of black-clad, visored figures peering in at the windows with blank glassy faces, reaching out for her with gauntleted hands.

Carla had to work harder at it, but she still knew how to win a smile, how to soothe her into quietness.

"Shall I tell you a story?"

Gwen wriggled happily and nodded.

"Once upon a time there was a family who lived in a big bus." Gwen never tired of this one.

"There was Mommy, and Daddy, and big brother Owen, and big sister Carla, and naughty David, and a little girl called . . ."

"Gwennie!"

All Carla's stories began this way. As the saga unfolded, and the adventures became more and more magical, Gwen drifted slowly into a comfortable doze, just awake enough to whisper a sleepy "and then what happened?" each time Carla paused to think.

She would never quite fall asleep until the story came to an end.

". . . and then they looked out over the sea, and there was the little boat coming back with Daddy and Gwennie and David in it, and it was loaded to the very top with treasure—gold and silver and all sorts of beautiful precious stones glowing every color of the rainbow in the sunset. So they ran and put the kettle on for tea, and they sat around the fire and told everyone all about how they had defeated the Dragon of the Eastern Isles and taken his treasure away, and Daddy said, 'Now we can buy our own farm in Wales and live on it for ever and ever,' but Gwennie said, 'Oh, no, Daddy, I want to stay in our old bus and have more adventures, because if we live on a farm all we'll have to do is grow potatoes and go to school every day.' And Daddy hugged her and said, 'All right, Gwennie, we'll do whatever you want.' And they did, and lived happily ever after."

Carla's singsong story voice sank to a murmur and died into silence beside her and sighed with satisfaction. Gwen stirred a little, but did not wake as Carla turned carefully onto her back and lay wide-eyed, staring at the outline of a window slowly becoming visible in the dawn light.

A faint sound jerked her from the edge of sleep into tingling wakefulness. The rattle of a dog's chain, the beginnings of a growl changing to a whine as a low voice spoke gently to it. Then the chain's rattle again. Carla could almost feel her ears prick. Faint and slow, stealthy footsteps crept away from the far side of the bus.

Mustn't wake Gwennie. Carla climbed carefully out of the bunk and felt in the dark for jeans and a dark-colored shirt. The emergency window at the end of the bus opened stiffly with a creak that sounded enormously loud. Barefoot, she clambered to the ground and crouched, leaning on the wheel. Her eyes already accustomed to the dark, she could see quite well. Dawn was barely lightening the sky beyond the dunes, but her eyes were already used to darkness. The black outlines of tents and vans were all familiar. At the outer edge of her vision something moved. She turned, stifling a sharply indrawn breath. At the far corner of the site the bushes seemed to hold the faintest impression of someone's passing. Stealthily, Carla rose to her feet and followed.

As she emerged onto the track two shadows flickered and vanished around a bend. Certain now of her quarry, Carla followed, up the beach road between sleeping bungalows towards the village. At the corner of the churchyard wall they turned down a narrow lane overhung by yew trees.

She hesitated under the thick, black branches, not wanting to come on whoever it was unawares. Perhaps it would be better to go back to the camp, get help. But then she might never find out who, and what, and why. Shuddering a little with apprehension and wincing each time her bare feet met sharp stones, keeping one hand on the old masonry of the churchyard wall, she inched forward until she came to a gateway.

There she paused, taking in the wide sweep of gravel and the imposing frontage of the pillared porch. Over to the left was what looked like garage doors. There they were! She crouched behind the stone gatepost, shrinking herself into concealment. Two shadows flitted back and forth, uncertain, searching.

Who were they? Stay hidden, take no risks. She slid slowly sideways among stiff laurel leaves that rattled at her touch. The soil was dry and powdery. She squatted down and watched.

A torch flashed briefly. A faint metallic scratching, and then, very slowly, the pale rectangle of the garage door narrowed and moved aside to make a dark opening. Two wraiths slithered between.

Silence and waiting. The growing light brought detail and colour but began to worry her. Her legs grew stiff and numb. She had to move to ease them, and every time the waxy leaves clattered. In spite of the tension, drowsiness fogged her mind.

The door closed quietly. She jerked awake in time to see two figures tiptoe rapidly across the gravel towards her. Immediately she recognized them. She stepped forward silently out of her hiding place and put a hand on Gary's arm.

"What the . . . Carla! What are you doing here?" Gary's voice was half-strangled with shock. Phil's arm shot out and checked itself only just in time to stop him sending her flying back into the bushes.

"What the heck are you doing?" Carla hissed back furiously. "Trying to get us all into trouble, aren't you? Don't you give a thought to what will happen to us?"

"Quiet!" Gary took a firm hold on her arm on one side and Phil's on the other. "If you stand here arguing we'll be in trouble all right. Get away from the village, then you can fight all you like."

Carla forced herself to silence. She could feel the anger boiling inside. She shook with it. How dare they? Endanger everyone when they'd been made welcome? They could go back to their other lives, do what they liked there. Travelers had to live with the reputation.

On the dune track, away from the houses, she could no longer hold it in.

"What did you do? You've got to tell me! You know we all get tarred with the same brush. If you've been stealing . . ."

Chris and Angharad had always been firm about that. Help yourself to things that nobody else wants—there were enough of them in this throwaway world—but never steal, not even when you know the owner has more than enough and won't miss it. The law will be twice as hard on you than the next person.

Gary, always more reasonable, tried to placate her.

"Don't you know whose house that is?"

Carla shook her head.

"That's where our precious Michael—the bike boy—lives. Now do you understand?"

"You've still got no right to get the rest of us into trouble. You did it on your own—you didn't ask anyone. You don't have the right when what you do affects the rest of us. What have you done?"

"Nothing very drastic. Don't you worry about it. We haven't broken anything, just made his bike a bit difficult to ride. Just as a warning. Nothing he won't be able to put right in five minutes. That's if he knows any more about bikes than how to roar about scaring kids."

Phil fished in his pocket and held up a pair of spark plugs in each hand.

"Just borrowed these. They'll come in handy when we get our bike on the road."

"Is that all?"

"No. His tires could do with a little air—and one or two other things'll need adjusting."

They turned into the track to the camp, Carla walking in silence between the two of them, angry still, relieved that it had not been worse, apprehensive as to what would happen now.

"You should have asked."

"We don't have to consult your dad before we do what we want," Phil barked. "We came here so that nobody'd tell us what to do. We get enough of that at home."

Gary nudged him to be quiet.

"Never mind that. Don't worry, Carla. That lad had it coming to him. If he's got any sense he'll take it as a warning. We won't lie down and let him bully little kids. You think of your Gwennie."

He was quick, he had kept his eyes open, he knew how to touch her.

"Don't tell your dad, there's a good lass," he went on persuasively. "It's too late now, and they're worried enough as it is."

Carla sighed and shrugged hopelessly.

"All right. I just hope you haven't made things ten times worse. You don't know how that boy may react."

She thought of Jake, of fighting evil with good. How did you do it anyway? Good just didn't seem strong enough, but evil just bred more evil. Gary and Phil didn't care. They looked at one another, exchanging grins.

"We'll be ready for him, won't we, Gary?" Phil said exultantly.

As they pushed their way between the alders the sky behind the dunes was showing pale blue. No one stirred. Carla stooped to stroke Swift's head and he licked her hand. The boys dived into their tent with scuffles and quiet laughter, pleased with themselves.

The little cluster of temporary homes looked vulnerable, flimsy, easy to destroy.

Gwennie lay ruffled and peaceful, her mouth a little open, her dark eyelashes delicate on her cheeks. Carla sat on her sister's empty bunk and waited for full morning, hunched, wakeful, and aching inside.

Warnings

11

The ripples of Michael's fury reached only slowly to the outer margins of Sea Norton. Perched on the edge of their cornfield and shut off from neighborly contact, Jeanie and her mother were about as far out as you could go. Jeanie tranquilly cleaned the house that Sunday morning, singing quietly to herself, while the village buzzed with outrage. Mrs. Richardson went to the morning service in the church and passed the news to Mrs. Dillon, who came in twice weekly to do her cleaning. Mrs. Dillon had always been so fond of young Michael. She was also sister-in-law to Mrs. Palmer at the shop. By the time the first late season day-trippers stopped off at the shop for ice creams on their way to the beach in the strengthening sun, everybody knew that Michael's motorbike was irreparably damaged. What was more, everybody knew who had done it.

"You want to watch out, down there on the beach," Mrs. Palmer was saying to the eager young families with their buckets and spades.

"Mind you keep well away from those wicked gypsies along the back of the dunes. And make sure the kids don't go wandering off. You don't know what might happen to them. There's been dreadful damage done in the village last night," she added darkly, but then, realizing she might be driving away trade, "not that there's anything to worry about in the daytime. They look so innocent when anyone can see them, but when they get under cover of darkness . . ."

Mrs. Palmer shook her head, full of foreboding, and rang up their purchases on the cash register.

"And a bag of chips? That'll be two pounds eighty."

Suddenly everyone had a crime to report. Washing missing from lines. Pots of jam, put out for sale by the garden gate and no money left in return. A lost pet rabbit, a missing chicken, a mysteriously damaged boat.

"I watch them like a hawk when they come in the shop, I can tell you," Mrs. Palmer told her friend Elsie Arthur, who lived on the beach road. "You'll have to be careful, your house is as close to them as anybody's, and most of the neighboring places empty at this time of year."

"And to think I've been going out and leaving the door unlocked." Mrs. Arthur, a widow, was a gentle soul who never thought ill of anyone. "They could have come in and cleared everything out! Everything I own! I never thought . . . Those little children, though, they look so sweet, and when they come along the road with their sister looking after them, I always think what a nice family they are in spite of everything. Do you really think it could be them doing all these things?"

"Don't you go by appearances, Elsie, my love," Mrs. Palmer patted her hand encouragingly. "I know you; you'd give your last shilling to a stranger if you thought he was hungry. Don't trust them. You keep your doors and windows locked and don't open up to a soul. It's not just robbery you've got to worry about—there could be worse. Much worse."

She looked hard and knowingly at poor Elsie, whose mouth slowly dropped open as she took in the possibilities. She hurried off to bolt herself safely in her bungalow, bringing her cherished pots of geraniums onto the porch for safety.

Michael was adamant about not calling the police. Since the village constable had been withdrawn years back, and officers started coming out in squad cars from the town, no one in the village had had much faith in them anyway.

"They'll only come and take a look and then say we can't prove anything," he told his parents. "Those hippies will all cover up for each other, and they can't arrest all of them. Anyway, it's not as if there's any real damage done. I can put this right easily. Though goodness knows why they picked on me."

He sounded cool, tolerant, almost amused as he turned away to hunt on the garage shelves for a spare set of plugs. His mother thought how mature he was growing, to be able to be so reasonable when he loved the bike so much. As a little boy he had been inclined to fly into a rage when anyone got in his way. It had worried her at the time, thinking what he might turn out to be. But he had grown up to be such a nice boy after all.

He went into the garage and shut the door. After drinking the last drops from the cola can in his hand he crushed it hard between his fingers, dropped it on the floor, and smashed it flat beneath his heel. But it gave him no satisfaction. He picked up a rag, turned to his bike and began rubbing and polishing every inch that they might have touched, rubbing and rubbing until it shone.

How dare that filth come here—into his home—and lay so much as a finger on his glossy, beautiful steed? He knew who had done it, all right; he had seen their faces when he rode through the camp. White and scared they'd been then, acknowledging who had the power. But now they had crawled out of their stinking holes in the darkness and touched what was his. He would show them what happened to people who did that.

He spent the rest of the morning putting the bike in perfect working order. The engine purred or roared, obedient to his slightest touch on the throttle. Not a smear nor a fingerprint marred its black and silver shine. In the afternoon he rode out in the direction of the town.

* * *

At last Jeanie's mood seemed to have begun to infect her mother, too. Today she was out of her dressing gown, though her dress was faded and crumpled and her hair hung in wispy, unkempt strands.

"I'll do the dishes."

When the doorbell rang she froze beside the kitchen sink, tea towel in hand, as if caught out in a guilty act. Small and thin like Jeanie, she had skin with the yellowish tinge of one who never went out in the sun. Her eyes, deeply shadowed by insomnia, flickered round the room, looking for a way of escape.

"Who do you think it is?" she whispered, dropping the towel to steady herself on the edge of the sink. She shuddered violently, and her breath began to come in gasps. Jeanie could see the panic coming on.

"Don't worry, Mom, I'll see to it." Jeanie guided her gently to the bottom of the stairs. "You go up and lie down for a while. I'll look after everything."

She watched her scuttle up the stairs like a frightened rabbit. Poor Mom—terrified of the world, terrified even of coming face-to-face with herself and what she had become. In her mind's eye Jeanie saw her as she had been before Dad died—laughing, hugging, the source of warmth and comfort. Now it was Jeanie who had to find strength for them both.

The bell pealed again, urgently. Jeanie tugged at the front door. They hardly ever used it, and it was swollen from moisture. It gave at last, swinging inwards with enough force almost to pin her against the wall.

"Jim!"

"I'm sorry, perhaps I should have come round the back. I wasn't sure."

He did look very unsure, standing on the weed-grown path. He glanced nervously around as if afraid that some-one would see him.

"Come in." Jeanie felt nervous too. She was not used to visitors. She led the way into the living room, hastily pulling back the curtains to let in the afternoon sun. The shabbiness and dust which was usually hidden by the half-light made her fell ashamed. But Jim saw none of it. His troubled gaze was fixed on her face. Looking at him, she knew better than to ask whether he had succeeded in speaking to Michael.

"I thought you ought to know—I mean, you don't get to hear what's going on in the village, and after what you came to me about yesterday . . . And people are saying you've been seen round with the hippie girl . . . They might . . . I mean . . ." Jim's face was knotted and contorted as painfully as his words. His misery touched her.

"It's all right," she reassured him. "I'm used to it. I don't care what they say. Carla and I are friends."

"No, you don't understand. You haven't heard. Something happened to Mike's motorbike last night. It was damaged. Someone got into the garage and let the air out of the tires and things. He's furious."

With cold certainty Jeanie remembered Gary and Phil, asking where Michael lived. And she had told them. Fear put its fingers around her neck and made it hard to breathe. Michael's anger . . . she had seen it before.

"What's he going to do?" she managed to ask.

"I don't know. He put the bike together and went off towards town. I didn't speak to him, but I saw him. He had that look on his face—you know? Not showing anything, but underneath he's so angry he can't do anything till he's let it out?"

Jeanie knew that look. She had tripped in the playground once, accidentally crushing Mike's new, shiny, toy racing car. All through afternoon school that cold, blank look bored into the back of her neck. On the way home, casually pinning her to the wall with one arm, he had emptied her school bag on the ground, stirring the contents with his toe until he found what he was looking for. A pair of tiny, painted wooden clogs that Dad had brought back from a trip to Holland. She loved those little clogs, and he knew it. Like blue rocks his eyes had been, as he ground the clogs into the earth with his heel. It was as if he was crushing her. After he had gone Jeanie knelt in the dust, trying uselessly to gather up the splinters of coloured wood that she could barely see through her tears. Jim had been there too, hanging awkwardly back behind his leader. Jim had been a coward then, just as everyone else had when it came to standing up to Michael.

"So I suppose you want me to warn them?"

She was challenging him. She wanted him, just this once, to take the right side, against Michael. He shifted from one foot to the other, twisting his shoulders uneasily.

"Well, it's up to you. I'm just telling you."

Suddenly Jeanie knew, to her surprise, who was the stronger of the two of them. Jim would be no help at all. He was right. She had to take control.

"You'd better go. You never know who might see you."

She couldn't resist the touch of irony, but it was lost on Jim. He was hurrying out of the still-open door and down the lane without even saying good-bye, back to the village and his small sphere of safety.

Jeanie sadly watched him go, her hopeful mood shrivelled and gone. The time for peacemaking was over, and now she had no choice about whose side to be on. She was alone. She had to make decisions and carry them out. If she failed, Jake was the only one she could rely on now.

Within the hour she was standing, a little out of breath, within the circle of the travelers' camp. The bus door was closed, so were the tents and Jo's van. No dogs leapt to greet her, no children ran from the dunes. A brown hen wandered clucking from the undergrowth, flies buzzed around a gnawed bone, the goat lay lazily in the afternoon heat. There was nobody there to warn.

Jeanie climbed to the top of the dune and surveyed the beach for as far as she could see. The tide was coming in. Families laden with bags and deck chairs were already making their way along the sand towards the car park, homeward bound. She strained her eyes, to make out a group of people far up the shore, where a haze was beginning to gather. Was it them? Those tiny specks gamboling in and out of the waves, could they be dogs? Or two small children? A taller figure walked away from the others towards the dunes. Chris! She was sure of it.

She dived down off the ridge and onto the narrowing strip of firm sand between the sandhills and the sea. Trotting first, then slowing to a walk, she set off up the beach as fast as she could go.

The Tomato Field

12

That morning Gary came looking for Carla as she walked along the high tide line, carrying a bundle of small driftwood for the fire. He wanted her to promise, again, not to tell anyone what she had seen in the night. His high spirits had worn off. She thought she could detect even a tinge of regret. Of the two of them, he was the more inclined to think before acting. Unfortunately, Phil's fiery moods all too often pulled both of them along. But he was right. The damage was done, and whatever resulted would happen anyway. There was enough tension in the camp as it was. All she could do now was to try and make sure it didn't happen again.

"OK. But this is the last and only time."

They had seen Chris angry, and it was enough to deter anyone. Besides, they weren't yet ready to go home. Satisfied, she went back with her load. There was little time for breakfast before they all left to walk the half mile inland to Bill Baines' farm.

Bill was an oddity in the neighborhood: a small land-owner who had taken to growing organic crops in order to make his acres pay, instead of selling out to the big landowners. When it came to the travelers he took no notice of local opinion. He owned the caravan site where they were allowed to get water, and when he had seasonal work he would call on them. Chris and Angharad were old friends—if it could be said that Bill had friends. He treated them the way he did everyone else, with terse respect.

"Dad used to get gypsies in," he had told Chris. "They did the work, came back year after year. Can't get them nowadays. Too many machines to make it worth them coming. They're being driven off the roads anyway. I can't afford machinery or permanent help. Rather have you than students. At least you work hard and don't grumble about the pay."

They were to bring his tomato crop in. The vines lay in a tangled mess on long, humped beds covered with black plastic sheeting. Each plant was pulled up by the roots and stripped, green and red fruit together, to be sent to one of Bill's organic cronies for chutney and ketchup. It was simple work that everyone could help with, even the children. The plants went onto a heap, the fruit into boxes which had been stacked ready at intervals down the edge of the field. The pay was so much a box. If they finished the field today, there would be a bonus.

It was backbreaking work, and the sun was getting hot. Bending, pulling, stripping—plant by plant, over and over and over again. The pungent smell of the tomato foliage clung to their hands and clothing. Carla wiped sweat from her forehead and felt it trickling down her back. She tried a different way of working, gathering a bundle of vines and sitting down by the hedgerow to strip the fruit. The change eased the ache in her spine. After a while they all tried it: Jo, Chris, Owen, Gary, and Phil pulling up the plants while the rest sat together picking. Then a change-over. It made the work go quicker, and those with the sitting job could talk. David and Gwen played in and out of the field, helping a little here and there, while baby Pippin slept blissfully on his stomach on a blanket spread in the shade.

Mid-morning, Mr. Baines turned up with his trailer to load the full boxes.

"Been a bit of trouble in the village," he grunted, muscles bulging as he raised an enormous pile. "Thieving, vandalism, they're saying. People blaming you. Just thought I'd let you know."

Carla glanced furtively at the boys and met Phil's eyes, fierce, defiant.

"Oh, people always blame everything on us," Angharad shrugged dismissively. Let trouble come to you, she always said, don't go looking for it. "They have to find a scapegoat. We're just the nearest outsiders, and there've been a few youngsters stirring things up of late. It's probably their doing."

Bill shrugged and got on with his work. It wasn't his job to protect anyone. They were adults. They could look after themselves.

Terry sat a little farther down the hedgerow, pulling tomatoes off and putting them carefully in her box. At Bill's words she stopped. Quite still except for her eyes, she sought out Sean's. She had found the morning's work hard. Her face, always pale and pinched, was clammy with the sweat of unaccustomed exercise. When the pickers changed jobs with the pullers, she and Sean worked apart from the rest, talking together earnestly.

By midday it was too hot to work in the sun. Under the overgrown hedge the grass had grown long. It was cool to sink into, cool and a little damp with its own crushed juice. Lying on her back, Carla watched the tall stems sway, and above them the soft scatter of light through hawthorn leaves.

"We've been thinking . . ."

Carla sat up. Sean and Terry were standing, hand in hand, stiff and formal before the pickers lounging in the grass. Earnest, slightly ridiculous because of his round, boyish face, Sean's words came out in a breathless rush.

"We'll be packing up tomorrow. Terry spoke to her cousin on the phone last night, and she says she can help us out for a bit. And with our share of money from today, we can manage till we look around for work."

Terry nodded for agreement, looking anxiously around the circle of faces as if afraid they might try to make her stay. Terry was like that. Always afraid. Carla tried to imagine what could have made her like that, but it was beyond her. Angharad somehow understood. She always did—that was why everybody came to talk to her, as Terry had, for hours and hours when they first arrived. She looked up at Terry now from the loaf and knife in her hands and smiled a smile that spoke something to her.

"We'll miss you," she said simply. "You've been a part of the family this summer, and we won't forget you. If you ever want to come back to us for a while, you'll always be welcome. You only have to ask round; you'll find where we are."

That was how the grapevine worked. Whenever travelers met, they exchanged news of others. If you wanted to get in touch, a friend of a friend of a friend would lead you there in the end.

Angharad patted Terry's hand.

"You'll be all right," she said. "Just keep believing in yourself."

Terry looked at Angharad doubtfully, her eyes shadowed and uncertain. But Sean's naturally open face broke into a grin.

"That's what I keep telling her. Everything'll be all right so long as we stick together." He looked shy all of a sudden, and younger than ever.

"We wanted to say thank you," he said awkwardly. "I don't know what we'd have done if you hadn't let us stay. And—you know—leaving us alone. We couldn't have gone back."

He put his arm around his girlfriend's shoulder and gave her a hard squeeze that was more embarrassment than affection. Nobody knew what to say. The girl looked around the group, her eyes flickering quickly to one and another, resting nowhere.

"It's not just because of the trouble in the village," she almost whispered. "We've got to go sometime, and it may as well be now, before it gets any colder." She was still anxious to please them, anxious not to appear to let them down. "And after a bit we'll need to get in touch with my Mom . . ."

Her voice trailed away into silence. Angharad put the

loaf aside and held out her arms. Kneeling, Terry went to them like a child. She seemed on the edge of tears.

"We'll miss you," Angharad said softly, then pulling away, "Anybody want a tomato?"

Everybody laughed.

By half past three the field was finished. Before they reached the last row, Bill Baines was stripping the perished plastic from the beds, heaping on rotted manure for the next crop.

"Good work," he yelled out, peeling off crumpled bills from a well-thumbed roll. "If you're still here, the other field next week. Take care."

The words were more than just a conventional phrase. He looked hard at Chris as he said them, but nobody else seemed to notice. Children and dogs ran ahead, cheerful at the release from work. They set off down a sandy path to the beach.

An east wind had begun to whip spume from the incoming waves. Sweat and grime and the yellow stink of tomato sap washed away, they felt exhilarated in spite of the chill of the water. Adults and children together forgot restraint, they leapt and chased and swam. Dogs ran in and out, barking with excitement, shaking themselves, snapping at flotsam in the shallow waves. Carla felt a great happiness that made her spin around in the water, head back, red hair streaming. Whatever threatened, moments like this no one could take away.

When Jeanie came half-running, half-stumbling up the beach and stood breathing hard, nobody noticed her. She shouted, but the strengthening breeze blew her words away. At last she splashed into the edge of the sea to grab at Carla's cold, wet arm and shout in her ear. Carla turned, startled. Her friend's face was strained and urgent, her eyes pleading, even fearful. Joy all lost, she let Jeanie pull her from the sea. Suddenly she was very cold, her body racked with spasms of violent shivering.

The others gathered around, tugging at towels, rubbing goose-fleshed arms and salt-stiffened hair. Above the noise of the wind and waves, Jeanie had to raise her voice.

"I think he really will do something," she ended. "Jim knows him well. If he wasn't worried he wouldn't have come. Michael's probably looking for more than just the gang you've seen. There are plenty of them with bikes, looking for trouble. You must do something."

Jeanie was clutching Carla's arm so hard that it hurt her. Her teeth were chattering, though not with cold. Chris and Angharad had moved closer together, the small children beside them. Owen, frowning, fondled his dog's ears. Gary and Phil, a little to one side, exchanged glances. Terry held on to Sean's arm, the fear coming out from hiding in her eyes. Jo asked:

"Have you any idea when they might make an attack? Surely not in daylight?"

"I don't know." Suddenly Jeanie felt deathly tired. What was the point of questions? She pushed them away. "He could do anything. I've told you what I know. You'll have to do what you think is best."

She sat down on the sand, the need for rest overcoming everything else. There was a scramble for clothes, snatches of conversation. She didn't want to listen. When, within minutes, the party set off almost at a trot, she sat and watched them go. She had done what she could, they didn't need her any more. Look at them, a tight knot of people drawing together to defend themselves. Even Carla had forgotten her.

The tide had covered the firm sand and walking on the soft, crumbly strip at the top of the beach was too much for her tired legs. She climbed slowly to firmer ground in the dunes. She recognized the place. It was here that she first met Jake.

She wanted him now, she needed his strength to lean on. Without hesitation she changed direction and headed straight for where he lived.

The Battle in the Dunes

13

What do you want me to do, Jeanie?"

She had found him seated again at the lathe, peacefully absorbed in his work. She staggered in the doorway, weak with exhaustion and relief. He had leapt to his feet, seeing her, with an exclamation of concern, to support her by the elbows and guide her to sit on an upturned crate. For the first time that day, she dissolved in tears. He sat patiently, offering the inevitable handkerchief. Then, hugging herself to try to stop the shivers that ran through her, she told him everything.

"I tried, I really tried—but it was no good. I wanted to stop all this from happening, but whatever I do is no use. Oh, Jake, why do people have to be like that?"

When he didn't answer she looked up into eyes dark with anger. It startled her, but at the same time her heart leapt. He must care a lot about her, he really must, to be so angry on her behalf. Then she was ashamed of the thought. That was the thing about Jake—he cared about people, and she was just one among many.

He turned his back abruptly and stood very still and tense. She had seen a hare like that, with its great ears pricked, motionless in the middle of a field. When he finally spoke it was as if the energy of his anger had changed course somewhere inside him and turned into a new purpose.

"What do you want me to do?"

It was not for this that she had come. She had run to Jake to get away, to bury her pain in his tranquility, to let him take control so she didn't have to be responsible any more. But he wasn't allowing her to do that. He was asking her to move on, giving the initiative back to her. It was all backward.

Jake waited for her reply. She could not run away. She saw it clearly now. She belonged in the village, and the travelers had become her friends. She might not be able to stop the conflict, but, like it or not, she was part of it.

"Could you come back with me?" she asked hesitantly.

He smiled. It was what he had wanted her to say.

"Don't expect too much of me," he said gently. "If you couldn't do anything, I probably can't either. I'm not Superman, you know."

"But you—we—could be there."

"Yes."

They went back the way she had come, down a track between hedgerows to the sea. Sheltered from a breeze, butterflies sunned themselves on the warm sand. Fear seemed far away. Jake strode purposefully, his long legs covering the ground so fast that Jeanie had to trot a few steps every now and then in order to keep up. His face was serious, almost grim. She felt a little in awe of him.

"It isn't safe for you to go to the camp," he said

abruptly as they approached the dunes. "We'll make a detour."

She accepted his authority without question. They turned off the track and climbed the ridge until they could approach the camp from the side nearest the sea. Looking down, they saw the travelers' home prepared for war.

A few hundred yards to their left a slow line of tourists' cars moved patiently up the beach road: tired, contented families heading for home. Below them lay the barricades. Vehicles drawn into a tight defensive formation, the log seats from the camp fire rolled to guard the gaps. Farther out, mounds of prickly brushwood barred the places where the bushes thinned, especially the gap where, last time, the bikes had broken through.

Chris, balanced on a trestle, was boarding up the bottom halves of the windows. Carla and Angharad had the hens shut in their traveling coop, cackling loudly as they were manhandled aboard the bus. Sean and Terry stood on the worn square of grass where their tent had stood, pushing poles and canvas into bags. Phil and Owen squatted in the long grass among the young trees, busy with something invisible. Everything that could move had been tidied away.

A movement on the dunes towards the village caught Jeanie's eye. On the end of a stick a red flag waved. The small figure of David was outlined against the sky for a moment, then disappeared. Far down the track towards the village she glimpsed an answering wave. Gary and the motorbike were missing. The sentries were already on duty.

Jake and Jeanie shifted from the skyline to where they

could sit concealed among buckthorn bushes, whose orange berries gleamed in the lowering sun. The camp was quiet now. Voices came faintly to them as the strengthening sea breeze snatched them away. There was nothing to do but wait.

Inland, the flat fields stretched for miles, divided by no more than a change of color where stubble gave way to plough and plough to shiny green beet leaves. The church spire of the next village, two miles away, stood up finger-like among its protecting trees. A narrow lane zigzagged crazily towards them along the field boundaries, marked by its double hedgerow. It looked so peaceful—no one was to be seen in all that landscape open to the sky.

A single moving speck emerged from far away beyond the trees, sliding along the tops of the hedges like a bead strung on a wire. Then another, and another—four, five, six—Jeanie stopped counting as the faint, unmistakable whine of motorbike engines came gustily to her with the slackening of the wind.

Jake felt her stiffen and followed her pointing arm. Together they looked back at the camp, still and unsuspecting. Jake's restraining hand was on her shoulder. There was nothing they could do. The watch had been set the wrong way.

The bikers—eight of them clearly visible now—with the sun glinting on their visors, heads down, came on fast in close formation, leaning into the corners, revving up in the straights.

Surely they must be heard now. She heard a faint shout. The first of the motorbikes left the metalled road and roared in a spume of sand up the track, tearing shreds of leaf from the bushes as it passed. It was Michael. In spite of the helmet she knew him from the lean, muscular hunch of his shoulders over the handlebars. It was Michael who burst out of the encircling greenery to roar triumphantly between the remaining tent and Jo's blue van, heading straight for the impudently multicolored bus. It was Michael, a moment later, who soared in a terrifying arc to hit the sand with a thud as his gleaming machine slid sideways, crashed to the ground, and lay with wheels helplessly spinning, like a scorpion viciously crushed.

One by one, the other bikes coming close behind swerved and screeched to a halt. As the engines died to sudden silence, for a moment everything froze. Then Michael moved, rolled over and sat up, gasping for breath, dazed, fumbling with the straps of his helmet. One of the others dismounted, ran to him. The doors of the bus opened and there was Chris.

"Now will you leave us in peace?" His voice echoed into the silence. At the back of the black-leathered group there was a small movement. One of the bikers, already, was preparing to leave.

Michael was on his feet now, bareheaded, defiant, shaking out his golden mane of hair. But no words came. The breath had been knocked out of him. He waved arms, ridiculous. It was Chris' moment of triumph. Perhaps he should not have smiled.

Behind Michael a powerful, thickset man, dressed in black leathers painted with a silver skull, quietly dismounted and walked deliberately towards the bus. He kept on walking until he was only a few inches from the door. Chris backed up a step. The man was huge.

Skull began to shout a stream of insult and obscenity. Chris stood still. Even at a distance, Jeanie could see the tension in his body as he controlled anger, the tiny glance over his shoulder, reminding him of those he wanted to protect.

He said something, but his words were lost on the wind. Two more bikers left their machines and ran forward. Several were shouting now. Behind them one crouched, paused, and threw something. Jeanie screamed a useless warning as a stone cracked against the bus doorway just above Chris' head.

Chris slammed the door as a second missile shattered a back window. Immediately, from up on the dune, a volley of stones, driftwood, rubbish hailed down on the attackers. Jeanie saw startled faces turned towards her, visors pulled hastily down as they ducked for cover. From their sand hollow high on the ridge, Owen and Phil began to pick their targets more carefully, reserving their ammunition. The bikers groped on the ground, searching for anything they could hurl in return. Jake pulled Jeanie down, flat on the sand. The battle had begun.

She didn't want to watch. She buried her face in her arms, unable to stop herself from hearing. The crash of breaking glass, again and again. Angry shouts, thuds, clangs, yells, and running feet. Far away, faint and muffled, the heartrending sound of Pippin crying. The new voices, men's voices, loud and angry. Slowly the thuds and crashes stopped. Jake's hand touched her shoulder.

"It's OK now." She edged forward and looked down on the battlefield.

Village people had appeared from nowhere. Mr.

Crocker, the publican, a huge man with a black beard and massive hairy arms, had Skull in a wrestler's grip on the ground. Mr. Palmer and two of his friends were climbing purposefully up the dune. Three heads—Owen, Phil, David—appeared with hands upraised in ironic surrender. Tom Benton, Jim's dad, weatherbeaten and wiry, had Michael firmly by the arm. Others, bikers and villagers alike, stood looking dazed and uncertain. One or two were mopping blood from faces or rubbing at limbs, but no one seemed badly hurt.

A car drew up. Dr. Richardson came into the clearing with his doctor's bag in his hand, looking professionally around for casualties.

"Is anybody . . ."

Father and son faced each other across a few feet of ground littered with broken glass. Michael had his back to her, but Jeanie could see the doctor's face. Just for a moment horror, anger, and shame chased themselves across his features, then it was as if a blind came down.

"Are you all right?"

Michael nodded. Dr. Richardson took in the crumpled machine.

"Tom, would you help him get that bike home?"

Angharad appeared in the bus doorway.

"You're a doctor? There's someone in here who needs your help."

Father and Son

14

Without another glance at his son, Dr. Richardson headed straight for the bus. Suddenly it was very quiet, like watching television with the sound turned off. Obediently Michael followed Mr. Benton towards the village. One by one the bikers collected their machines and wheeled them away. The village men gathered in an uncertain knot, looking curiously around and muttering together, like guests come too early for a party. Phil, climbing down from the dune with Owen and David, went to the trees at the entrance to the camp and began untying and coiling the thin strand of wire which had been Michael's downfall.

The sound of a motorbike caused them all to turn, but it was only Gary, turning in slowly and coming to a halt by the tent, accosting Phil with eager questions, obviously disappointed at having missed the fight.

Jim pushed his way through the bushes and stood staring at the devastation, his tanned face pale and rigid. He looked lost. Jeanie came out of hiding and went to meet him.

"Was it you who brought the men here?"

"Sort of. I was with my dad at the slipway. We heard

the noise, and I knew what must be going on. He fetched the others."

Jim spoke in an undertone, staring at his feet, unwilling to meet her eye. Jeanie, understanding, reached out a tentative hand to his arm.

"You did what you could, Jim," she said. "You were right, you know. He wouldn't have listened to you."

She felt tense muscles relax a little beneath her fingers as he turned to her with a pleading face.

"D'you really think so? I'm a coward, Jeanie—I chickened out. I could have gone to him last night. I didn't have the guts. I kept thinking I'd do it in the morning, and then it was too late. I'm so pathetic. After this, I don't know what I ever saw in him."

"He was your friend. You go back a long way."

"Yes."

Dr. Richardson came striding across the open ground.

"No one hurt, I'm glad to say, though that young girl with the fair hair had a touch of hysterics. The other woman wouldn't let me give her any sedative. Said something about brewing up camomile tea. Can't do any harm, I suppose, these old country remedies."

He nodded cheerfully at Jeanie.

"I'm glad you weren't caught up in it."

She could hardly believe it was the same man. Only a few moments before, shock and grief had sat so plainly in his face. Now he was acting as if she was the one in need of comfort. Did he think she hadn't seen? How stupid he was, this man she had respected all her life because he was supposed to know what was good for her. Did he think what had happened could be ignored, brushed under the carpet as if it didn't change their lives, and especially his?

But she couldn't say any of this to him. It wasn't just that she was Jeanie the epileptic, her mother's daughter, an object of pity. It wasn't just that she knew he wouldn't listen. It was as if there was a barrier in her throat stopping the words from coming out. The desperation she felt for Michael flooded over her so strongly that she couldn't say a word. She looked back to where they had sat on the dune. *Help me, Jake,* she was saying silently. And there he was, coming quietly to her side.

"Dr. Richardson," she heard herself saying. "I want you to meet Jake."

Jake held out his hand, bowing gawkily in his old-fashioned courteous way. The doctor's hand responded out of habit, as if its owner didn't want it to. Jeanie could see him trying to assess the stranger.

"You're with this group of . . . visitors?"

"No. I live alone. Jeanie and I have become friends. When she found out what was happening she asked me to come along."

Dr. Richardson was totally at sea. "Friends?" What did the man mean? He glanced suspiciously from Jeanie to Jake and back. Not a local man—he knew everyone in the area. And what an extraordinary looking chap. Jeanie had had such an odd, sheltered life. Surely she knew not to trust him—or was she too innocent? And yet the man had such an air of straightforwardness about him, as if he expected you to take every word he said precisely at its face value.

Jeanie smiled inwardly. Jake had spoken the truth, but

it was so hard for the doctor to understand. There were further shocks to come.

"Dr. Richardson," Jake was saying, looking straight into the man's face in a way he found most disturbing. The expression in his eyes he could only describe as love. His words came out with a passionate urgency. For a few moments the doctor was persuaded to listen.

"I realize you know nothing about me and have no reason to trust me, but please listen for a moment, because what I say is true. You must help your son before it's too late. He's in danger. He has put himself under the influence of evil. If he is to get free, you must isolate him from these men, and especially from their leader. And even that is not enough. He needs help to overcome the love of power which has brought him into this. There is only one power that can overcome evil . . ."

"That'll do!"

The doctor's eyes were snapping with fury.

"I'm a scientist, Mr. . . Jake. You can't expect me to listen to this medieval nonsense. And as for how I treat my son, it's none of your business."

He turned sharply on his heel, almost too angry to speak. Then after a few steps he turned again.

"And I suggest you keep away from this girl," he went on more quietly. "She's a vulnerable child, trusting and easily influenced. As I expect you know only too well. I'd like you to know I shall be keeping my eye on her. If you dare take advantage . . ."

He turned to Jeanie.

"You heard what I said. If you have any sense you'll

keep clear of this man. Not only will he fill your head with dangerous nonsense, you have no reason to believe he can be trusted. You're old enough to know what I mean."

He nodded to himself, satisfied that his duty had been done, then threw his bag into the car and himself after it. Jeanie, recovering rapidly from astonishment at his reaction, ran after him, knocking on the window until he wound it down.

"It's all right, Dr. Richardson. Please don't worry about me. You don't understand at all. Jake's not like that. He's the best friend I ever had. He wouldn't ever touch or hurt me."

She faltered for a moment, because all her loving feelings for Jake suddenly woke up in her. It wasn't quite true, what she was saying—not on her side.

"He wouldn't—not even if I wanted him to," she managed to blurt out.

His eyebrows shot up comically in surprise at her outburst. Already putting the car into gear, he put out a hand and patted the one that rested on the car door.

"Just be careful, Jeanie, dear. People aren't always what they seem. You'll learn that as you grow older."

She stood looking after him, not knowing whether to laugh or cry. He really hadn't the faintest idea what her life had been like, how much older she sometimes felt than people like him.

Jake came and stood silently beside her. She looked into his face; it seemed older, sadder than she had seen it, a look that wrung her with the desire to comfort him.

"He's like that, Jake. It can't be helped."

"I know." He sighed, smiling down at her but with the sadness still in his eyes. "It's not that, Jeanie. I don't expect people to accept what I say, especially when it's a hard word. It's Michael that causes me pain." He looked slowly round at the devastated campsite. "Michael, and all these people too."

There was something he knew that she was unable—and didn't want—to know. It was as if for a moment an island of cold fog engulfed them alone in the midst of the sunny afternoon.

Then Angharad brought them tea and an invitation to join the others round the rekindled fire.

"My daughter has told me about you," she said to Jake, drawing up her small form with matriarchal dignity. "Thank you for coming."

"You must thank Jeanie for bringing me," Jake answered gravely. "I'm sorry there wasn't anything I could do to stop this happening. Another time, if it should come to that, I may be able to."

Angharad looked at him oddly, this scarecrow-man who seemed to think he was responsible for them, but it was her way to accept odd people. She thanked him once again.

The broken glass and scattered missiles took little time to clear away. Apart from the broken windows Jeanie could have believed nothing had changed since she had sat here only a few days before. Though that day, Jeanie recalled heavily, had been the beginning of it all.

"We did for him good and proper this time, didn't we?" Gary greeted her exultantly. "That was his dad, wasn't it? The doctor? He'll be none too pleased to find out what his precious son's been up to. I just can imagine . . ." He chuckled in anticipation.

"We've no reason to be celebrating, except that we're all safe and well," Angharad broke in. Her usually soft voice was bitter, and her green eyes flashed. Today's events had shaken her. Her optimism was all gone.

"What happened today won't make the village people love us. It was one of theirs that did it, and they won't even admit he's in the wrong. They'll say it's our fault in the end. It would probably save a lot of trouble if we packed our bags before they get the police to turn us off."

"But that would be giving in, Mom," argued Owen fiercely. He had her eyes, and they were as bright with passion.

"We can't let them drive us away. We've got a perfect right to be here. Can't you imagine them laughing at us? It'd be exactly what they want."

Chris, putting a restraining hand on his son's shoulder, took up a commanding position by the fireplace and spoke in measured tones.

"You're right in one thing. Legally they can't send us off. Only the owner of the land can do that, and it just so happens that nobody knows who the owner is. Years ago, the local landowner sold off this strip along the dunes. Several people bought plots for holiday bungalows, but then the planning laws came in and they weren't allowed to build. Since then some have died and their land has changed hands, and even if the owner of this particular patch could be found, he might not be interested enough to take action against us. The police can't do anything.

Until the owner says otherwise, no one can evict us. Young Michael and his friends can make it hard for us—but that's another matter. As you say, Owen, packing up would only encourage them. My vote is for staying."

He turned to Jeanie. "Would you keep in touch with any developments? It would help us decide what to do."

She nodded automatically. The conversation swept onward, ignoring her. She felt drained. She had fought so hard and achieved so little. Wouldn't it have been better to have left well enough alone? The bikers would have found the camp empty. They could have damaged things, but no one would have been hurt. It might even have been better in the end.

So she had exposed Michael to his family, to the village. Would anything come of it? Had she done anything good? Or just stirred up more evil? *There's only one power that can overcome evil . . . , Jake had said. What did he mean?* She felt utterly powerless, confused. Questions revolved dizzily in her mind. Did she even know what was right, wrong, good, evil? One action, so many mixed results. Jake was so sure: he saw black and white where for her there was only gray. If only she could believe he was right.

Her head drooped and she jerked suddenly awake again. Jake's arm steadied her, then firmly pulled her to her feet.

"I'm afraid I must take Jeanie home," he was saying. Dimly she took in Carla's whispered thanks. As they took the fields home, the cool air and exercise slowly revived her.

"You must come in and see my mother," she found herself saying impulsively at the gate.

"I will, but not today. You must give her time to be ready for me."

He was right, of course. Mom would be terrified if she brought a stranger home unexpectedly. Even with time to prepare her, Jeanie could not be sure how he would be received. Yet if anyone could help her, she found herself suddenly sure of it, Jake was the one.

"Come tomorrow, then, when I get home from school."

She undid the latch of the gate, then turned back to him, letting it fall again.

"Jake?"

"What is it?"

"When you try to do what seems right and it doesn't work out, what do you do?"

He looked very straight at her, and she knew he had been where she was and knew exactly what she was asking.

"You trust, Jeanie. Just keep trusting that the one who invented right will bring it about in the end."

What did he mean? Just when she thought she understood he started saying things that made no sense to her. But Jake had nothing more to say. He watched her into the house, then turned and disappeared into the gathering darkness.

Revenge

15

We must do something to show we won't lie down and be trampled on."

It had grown dark around the fire. The last shards of glass had been carefully picked from the sand, the broken windows were boarded up. The children were in bed. Outwardly, order had been restored. But still Owen could not let the argument lie. At last Carla could no longer bear to keep the silence she had promised to Gary and Phil.

"We already have—or at least some of us did. And look where it got us."

"We were only defending ourselves this afternoon," Chris said, not understanding. "We had no choice. And what we did made things no worse, even if people choose to twist it round and blame us for violence."

Carla shook her head, staring at the boys across the flaring camp fire.

"That's not what I meant."

Jo, quick to catch the undercurrents of a conversation, followed the direction of her eyes, and saw Gary look up sharply, while Phil shifted uncomfortably in his seat.

"What do you mean? What did they do?"

"What d'you have to bring it up for, Carla?" Gary was indignant. "I told you there was no point."

"It affects all of us now. Are you going to tell them or shall I?"

He looked around the firelit circle gone suddenly very quiet, and shrugged, elaborately casual.

"I will if you like. I don't care what you say, I don't regret it."

He paused, enjoying the effect now he had their attention.

"We sabotaged the golden boy's bike."

Another pause. Nobody cheered.

"Last night. Nothing serious. Just one or two little alterations. Nothing that couldn't be easily fixed."

Finally, Sean spoke quietly for them all.

"You idiots."

"I've never done this before," Chris added slowly. "But I've a good mind to ask you to leave our company."

Owen's head came up sharply. Carla could see, sharply outlined in his features, the deep-down anger that made him ready to take sides against his father.

"Why do you all say it was their fault? We hadn't done anything to him when he knocked Gwennie into the brambles, or when they came here before. We don't know what might have happened. He hates us anyway, just because we're here."

"When a wild animal is about to attack you, Owen, the last thing you do is provoke it." Chris never raised his

voice, but his logic came down like a hammer-blow.
Owen flushed at the humiliation.

"So what do you do? Run away?"

"Perhaps. It may yet come to that. There's no shame
in withdrawing when you know you can't win. But as I
said earlier, not just yet, at least as far as our family is
concerned." He looked around the circle of firelit faces.
"The rest of you, of course, will do as you think best. Sean
and Terry have already decided to go. How about you,
Jo?"

"We'll stay on. I can get out in a few minutes if I have
to. I've faced worse than this. Though then I didn't have
Pippin to think of."

Owen, dismissed and ignored by his father, said nothing more. But Carla was watching when Chris extracted
a promise from Gary and Phil not to provoke more
trouble. A small smile flitted across his shadowed features,
and she knew what was in his mind. Nobody made him
promise. As the circle broke up for the night he slipped
away to the beach with Swift. Carla followed his dark
shadow in the moonlight.

"Owen!"

He whipped round, alert and suspicious.

"It's all right. Only me."

She came close to him, and they walked together,
listening to the creaming surf, watching glints of light
playing on the water. Up the coast a lighthouse flashed a
rhythmic warning. The vastness of the dark sea calmed
her, as she knew it would calm Owen too. Wait, she told
herself, let it work its spell. He'll listen to me then. Swift

ran up the beach and back, pausing at scents, splashing into the water, returning to his master like an erratically swinging pendulum.

"Owen, I know you're angry," she began at last.

"And I know what you're going to say," he interrupted her. "Everyone's been saying it for the last hour. Cool it, don't stir up trouble; we'll all get hurt. And let that jerk get away with it."

He was calm all right, but the hatred was still there, the more frightening for its coldness. Imperceptibly Carla moved away from him as if fearful of contamination. Anger she could understand—at the injustice of it all, at being a victim. There was something right about that. But this . . . this Owen she felt she had never known.

"Just think of the kids," was all she could say, lamely, knowing he would take no notice. "It's Gwennie. You know what she's like."

"OK, OK. I've heard it all. Don't worry. Nobody's going to get hurt, except possibly me. And that Michael."

He looked sideways at her, bending to fondle Swift's ears as the dog came back to his side. In the dark she was sure he was smiling, but his voice was harsh and humorless. Chris had driven him to this, Carla realized. He hadn't meant to. He hadn't understood how proud and sensitive his son was. And once Owen made up his mind, there was nothing even Chris could do to stop him.

"Be careful."

"Don't worry."

Don't give back evil for evil, Jake had said, and the

words rang longingly in her mind. But, in spite of herself, a part of Carla wished Owen well in his revenge.

None of them slept very well. In the morning Angharad had a kettle on, and those who were awake were gathering by the fire, bleary and aching, when Jeanie wobbled into the camp on a bicycle too small for her. News from the village, she panted. A poster had gone up in the shop. There was a meeting tomorrow night in the parish room. Everyone invited, to discuss "unauthorized squatting." Must go, the school bus would be here any minute. She'd be back this evening, and could she bring Jake?

By mid-morning Jo had taken Sean and Terry in her van into town to the station. Carla tried not to look at the stained yellow patch where their tent had been. Only a few days ago she had waked to a morning made for dancing. Now she only wanted to sit hunched on her bed, wrapped in a blanket against the drafts that pierced the window-boarding. Overnight, autumn had come. The wind off the sea brought without warning a stinging, drenching rain.

By afternoon, weak sunshine struggled through the clouds. Tired of the bus and even of Gwennie's demands for games and stories, Carla wandered up onto the dune to watch the sea. The damp air crept through her jeans, but she needed to be alone, to shake off the heaviness that dogged her. Swift followed, whining, and settled with his head on her knees. She stroked him absently, glad of the comfort. It was some time before she wondered why he was not with Owen. Where Owen went, Swift went too, and Owen was not in the camp. She realized with a twinge of dread that she knew, yet did not know, where he had gone.

It was late in the day when he limped home. He was filthy. Blood from his nose smeared his face and stained his shirt. But his face showed a mind at rest and satisfied. He had fought Michael bare-handed, and won.

"I hung around the house until I saw him go out. On foot. I expect he's not allowed to use the bike anymore. He went for a walk along the dunes on the other side of the village, by himself—a sitting target. I followed. When we were well away from anywhere I jumped him. He may be bigger than me, but he's soft. A soft bully. He did this"—he touched his nose tenderly—"but I did worse to him."

He had what he wanted; he had his revenge. Even Chris' ice-cold anger couldn't pierce the armor of his content.

"You realize you'll almost certainly be charged with assault? You've stepped over the line, Owen. Up to now we've been on the right side of the law. We could claim protection, even if we didn't get it. Now you've put us where no one can defend us."

Only Jo took his side.

"You know quite well the law will do nothing for us," she told Chris, flaring with indignation. "Owen's justice is better than any we'll have from the system." She swept off to her van before anyone could argue.

Carla took in what Owen had done and it was like iced water pouring down her spine. Surely now there was no hope. But her brother was like a child playing with fire, gleeful, delighted with his conflagration.

"You should have seen his face," he chuckled painfully, as Carla helped him, leadenly, to bathe his swollen nose and wash blood from the graze on his cheek. "He was terrified when I had him on the ground. You know, I think he was even afraid I was going to kill him. He thought I was a savage, a wild man. I don't reckon anyone's ever stood up to him before. He's always had his own way. I don't care if I do get arrested. It was worth it, just to see him as frightened as he made us."

Owen couldn't bear the way the bikers had made him afraid. The humiliation of it. And now he really couldn't see what he had done.

None of them spoke much that evening. Supper was prepared, the animals fed and bedded, extra sleeping bags and blankets brought from storage against the night chill. The children squabbled irritably, and Angharad, exasperated, sent them to fetch water. Cooking supper, she dropped fat in the fire and burnt her hand. It was not like her to be clumsy. Pippin squalled and would not be comforted, setting all their nerves on edge.

As darkness fell, still no one had anything to say. It was too cold to sit outside, someone had said, and each felt secretly glad to crowd into the cramped security of the bus, away from the night at their backs. Jo brought out her guitar, but no one wanted to sing, and she sat bent over it, desultorily sampling chords. Angharad brought out clothes to mend, Chris a book. Owen, his euphoria wearing away, sat hunched sulkily in a corner, now and again raising a finger to test the tenderness of his rapidly-swelling face. Carla leaned back with Gwen drowsing on her lap, and closed her eyes wearily. Whenever a silence fell, they all found themselves listening.

When someone knocked on the door, Carla jumped so violently that Gwennie clung to her and whimpered in fear.

Home for Tea

16

Whatever had happened that day, Jeanie felt she would not have minded. When the world turned chilly, she could draw around herself a warm protective cocoon: the knowledge that Jake was coming to tea. But in fact the day turned out better than she could remember for a long time.

At the bus stop Caroline had plenty to talk about. Usually Jeanie timed her arrival so as not to have to pretend to ignore her snide comments.

"I washed my hair last night," she would say, stroking her silky blonde locks. "I got some new conditioner in town that really makes it shiny."

Then she would invite Jeanie to touch, half-closing her eyes with catlike pleasure and all the time implying, with sideways glances, that Jeanie's hair, with or without conditioner, could never be anything like hers.

But today her malice, thankfully, was directed elsewhere. Jeanie's part in the events of the weekend, evidently, had passed the gossips by. Caroline was indignant at the travelers, but that meant nothing to Jeanie. It hurt no one, and she could ignore it. Surprisingly, it was Dr. Richardson whom Caroline singled out for abuse.

"He gave Michael that bike, and he knows how much it means to him," she complained petulantly. "How can he lock it away from him? He hasn't the right. Poor Michael is so upset."

Jeanie could have said something about "upsetting" other people, but she didn't bother. She was glad that Dr. Richardson had taken some notice of what Jake said. Knowing that made putting up with Caroline a possibility.

On the bus, Caroline rushed to become the center of her gaggle of friends. Jeanie took her solitary seat, watching the familiar countryside and then the scatter of houses that heralded the town. Today she was comfortable with being alone. Without knowing it she walked lightly through the school gates, her head high, her shoulders straight and relaxed. The miserable hunch of previous weeks had completely disappeared.

Robert Wylie saw her and fell into step hesitantly beside her. She looked up at him with a smile. She didn't even feel awkward with him. She felt she could understand and forgive anything. It must have shown, because Robert's shamefaced look vanished at once.

"See you at lunchtime?" he said hopefully.

"OK."

Was that almost a skip in her gait?

Lessons were bearable if only they left her alone. Today none of the teachers singled her out. Even math, in her tranquil frame of mind, became understandable. The afternoon was art, the one thing she really enjoyed. All the time in her head ran the bubbling theme of happy anticipation. It did not occupy her thoughts, distract or confuse her mind. It was like the deep bass notes of a symphony, binding everything together. Concentration became effortless, ideas full of light and clarity.

"That's outstanding, Jeanie." Mrs. Jasper, the art teacher, looked over her shoulder. There was respect in her voice. She had known Jeanie had talent, but her work was always jerky, inconsistent, not flowing confidently from hand and eye.

Today she had drawn autumn sunlight slanting through golden leaves. The trees' branches moved in the wind, the light was mellow, delicately scattered. The warmth invited you in.

Jeanie smiled, saying nothing. She knew what Mrs. Jasper couldn't know. It was a picture of the way she felt about Jake.

After school she slipped across to the baker and bought a box of cakes, choosing carefully, delighting to do so. She would have to run to catch the homeward bus.

She would have to be quick to have everything neat and tidy before Jake came. At the back door she was surprised by a faint smell of baking in the air. No breakfast crockery in the sink, or even left to drain in the rack. No greasy stains round the taps, no crumbs on the worktop, no smears on the cupboards, no dirt on the windows— even the cracked floor was clean. Cups and saucers laid on a tray—the best china, with its rosebuds and gilt edges, that had sat dusty in a cupboard for two years. And the source of the smell—scones, golden and fluffy, cooling on a wire rack.

Jeanie reached out a finger to touch one gently. They were still just warm. She put down her box of cakes, flung her bag in the corner of the hall, draped her jacket on the coatrack.

"Mom!" she called with flooding excitement. "Mom! Where are you?"

Last night she had sat with Mom a long time. Her friend Jake was coming to tea, she had said. She must not be afraid of him. She knew Mom would like him, if only she would not be afraid. Please Mom, please try to do this for me. It's so important.

Mom had listened and nodded obediently, her eyes downcast, her hands twisting and untwisting her handkerchief. She would try.

"I'm upstairs, Jeanie."

She was running up as fast as she could go. This time there would be no stuffy darkened room, no huddled figure under the blankets, no smell of despair.

A woman was sitting at Mom's dressing table, brushing out her hair. She wore a dress that Jeanie remembered, a summer cotton dress, rather old-fashioned now, but pretty, with blue and yellow flowers and a lace collar. Memories of a long-ago summer, of a village fete, of Dad . . .

The face reflected above the dress in the mirror was not the face from long ago. That one had been fair-skinned and freckled with sun, light with laughter. This one was pale and hollow-eyed, and the color on the cheeks came out of a box. But it was a different Mom from yesterday.

It was as if shape and form had been subtly sculpted into the blankness of features eroded by despair. She turned stiffly, as if frightened to spoil the effect. The whole edifice was held together by pure determination. Jeanie knew, gratefully, that Mom had done it for her.

"How do I look?"

"Oh, Mom." Jeanie came close and knelt on the floor to put grateful arms around Mom's waist. For once there was no stiffening at her touch, no shrinking away. Instead, a hand came up and stroked her hair.

"When I woke up this morning I lay there thinking, I've got to get up for Jeanie today, and be ready for this friend she thinks so much of. I made myself do it. It's taken me all day, but I managed. And then the oddest thing happened. When I came up here and got this dress out of the cupboard I looked at myself in the mirror and I thought, *You're the same woman who wore this dress the day Dad was killed.* I've never believed that before. I thought everything had fallen apart, that nothing could ever be the same again. That there was no point in even trying to put things back together. But in that moment I knew it wasn't true. Dad can't come back. But I'm still me, and I've got you."

She seemed to be talking to herself, whispering things not voiced before. It was a very long time since she had said so much. Then she was quiet, and Jeanie had nothing to say. In the silence a sense of awe came over her, so that she was afraid to move for fear of breaking something. She was a child whose wildest dream has been fulfilled, whose frog has turned into a prince. It could not be understood, but it was wonderful.

Mom broke the spell with a little businesslike pat on her shoulder.

"Come on, you get out of that uniform. We must be ready when he comes."

Downstairs, the living room looked for once just that—no longer a dead room. Sunlight through the clean window showed up the faded furniture and threadbare carpet, but also sparkled on the rosebud china. The polished table glowed. A vase of yellow chrysanthemums was almost dazzling. Jeanie laid out her cakes with careful pleasure. Everything was ready.

As she opened the door to Jake, Mom came nervously into the hall, clutching the banister as if to stop herself from running away, pushing down, with an effort that cost her dearly, the old habit of fear.

"This is my mom, Jake."

He must have put on his best clothes—a pair of maroon trousers with scarcely a patch on them, though the style must have been fifteen years old, and a long, washed-out jumper in green and gold. For all his strangeness, his manners were of perfect courtesy.

As he stepped forward to take Mom's hand, he could have been meeting the Queen. Mom looked up at the towering figure and stood her ground. She gave him a small, brave smile.

Jeanie was so proud of her.

These are the two people I love most in all the world, Jeanie thought, looking from one to the other. A frail-looking woman in an old flowered dress, her face etched with the lines of two years' grief and loneliness, sitting upright on the edge of her chair and nervously sipping tea; and a scarecrow of a man in his motley suit, stretching his long legs as he leaned back in his chair, filling his mouth with buttered scones, and letting his dark eyes signal the enjoyment that seemed to mark everything he did.

Wherever he was Jake was completely at ease. Complimenting Mrs. Grant on her scones, on her excellent tea, he went on to have them laughing at a hilarious account of his attempts to make cakes on a wood stove. Within minutes Mom was beginning to unwind, to enjoy the simple pleasure of sitting here in her house and feeding tea and cake to a young man who appreciated her hospitality. Somehow or another, Jake made her feel that at that moment nobody else in the world could have given him such pleasure. She even began to feel young again.

Afterwards Jeanie couldn't remember what it was they talked about, but it must have been an hour before Jake stood up, brushing the crumbs from his lap.

"It's been such a pleasure to meet you."

He meant every word. Mom glowed as he took his leave of her. Jeanie followed him out to the porch.

"Can you come and see the travelers with me tonight? The village has organized a meeting. I said I'd go and help them decide what to do."

"And you think I can help?" He looked at her quizzically with eyebrows raised.

"Of course you can help. Look what you've just done for Mom."

He was serious then—very serious, looking at her and speaking slowly as if there was a lesson he wanted above all else for her to learn.

"I didn't do anything. I just blew in with the wind.

The wind blows wherever it pleases. You hear its sound, but you cannot tell where it comes from or where it is going. But you see where it's been."

Why did he talk in riddles? Jeanie could have shaken him.

"What do you mean, Jake? Why can't you explain?"

"When you're ready, Jeanie, you'll understand. Things hidden from the wise in this world are revealed to the weak and foolish. You'll understand. I'll see you at the camp later."

He was gone. She stared after his gaunt figure stalking up the road. What was he talking about? It was as if he had a secret he wanted her to share, but wouldn't explain. And why did it seem, sometimes, that he was speaking words that were not his own—half-familiar, like quotations from Shakespeare?

In the kitchen Mom was singing softly as she cleared the dishes away. Jake spoke the truth: it was as if a fresh, gentle wind had breathed through the house and all the black, sticky cobweb-things of the past had been blown away.

War and Peace

17

C hris moved to the door and slipped the chain into place before cautiously opening it a crack. Angharad, curled up in the corner of the bunk, put an arm around David's shoulder. Carla clutched at Gwennie and felt her arms go tight around her neck. Jo put down the guitar and gently picked up the sleeping Pippin who whimpered faintly. Owen froze in his corner on the floor, the color draining from his bruised face. Gary and Phil, with a quick glance at each other, moved forward on either side of the boy, half-crouching, to conceal him from the intruder.

Carla felt a shiver go down her spine as a man's voice answered her father's challenge.

"May we come in?"

From behind she saw Chris' shoulders let go their tension. He stood back, releasing the door and allowing the lamplight to fall on the faces of Jake and Jeanie at the bottom of the steps. Angharad stood at once to welcome them, her red hair flowing, the blanket wrapped around against the evening chill making her look like a diminutive barbarian queen.

"We're nervous tonight," she apologized. "There's

fear about, and we seem to have let it in. It's done us no good, making us suspicious of friends. Please come in."

There was a general shuffling around of seating in which the defensive positions of Gary and Phil were easily abandoned without remark. Four of them squashed into the bunk, Jake took the one armchair with Jeanie perched on its arm, while the rest squatted on the floor. Angharad's offer of tea was accepted, and Owen was sent outside to fill a kettle and blow on the embers. It gave Chris the chance to explain what had happened that afternoon.

"So you were afraid we might be the police?" Jake asked.

"Or worse."

They all knew what that meant. Jeanie's eyes met Carla's and saw fear in them.

"Knowing Michael," Jeanie said thoughtfully. "I should think the police are unlikely. He'll be very angry, but mostly from humiliation. He never could bear to be beaten. He won't admit to his parents what happened. He'll probably make up a story about how he got hurt, and then look for another way of getting back at you."

It was not a comforting thought. After all, last time she had underestimated Michael. He wasn't, any more, the child she had known. And his chosen friends were much more alarming.

Owen returned with the steaming kettle and a can of milk. Angharad found mugs in a cupboard, poured water in the pot. They were thankful to shut the door on the rapidly-gathering darkness.

Jeanie could not help drawing a parallel with this

afternoon's tea at home. Not just the chipped mugs instead of bone china, or the cramped informality instead of polite convention. The feel of it was utterly different. The lightness and grace she had carried around all day was being slowly smothered. Nobody smiled. In nine pairs of eyes lurked a physical fear that nobody wanted to admit. All of those eyes, for some reason, were fixed on Jake as if he were their only hope.

Yet Jake was as much at home as he had been in the Grants' living room. Though now he was serious, staring thoughtfully into his mug as he stirred his tea.

"So you'd really like to stay on?" he asked Chris directly, eye-to-eye, expecting as direct a reply.

"For this year, it doesn't really matter. We generally leave around the end of September. But it's a good place to spend the summer, and if we leave with the village against us we won't be able to come back next year. They'd have time, over the winter, to find the owner and have him fence it off. Then it'll be lost for good, and not just to us. Another piece of land barricaded off, lying useless like so many others, just because somebody owns it."

A note of bitterness crept into the tall man's voice. Jake heard and answered it.

"You feel you have a right to this place. And the villagers want to take it away from you. It's as much a matter of principle as of convenience."

"Of course. Don't they always? We only want to live alongside them in peace, but can they accept that?"

He shook his head, then went on, warming to his

theme and thumping a hand on the table to emphasize each point. Anger blazed in his eyes as he struggled to keep his voice from rising to a shout.

"People like that run true to form. They're normal; we're peculiar. Therefore we shouldn't be allowed to exist. Everything we do must be wrong. In their eyes, we've caused the trouble. If we hadn't been here, it would never have happened. Never mind who started it, it's our fault. It's always the same. Blame the scapegoat, point the finger. They couldn't possibly be responsible.

"Look at the way they tried to pin every petty crime in the last three months on us, just because those two were stupid enough to mess around with that young bully's bike. There's no changing people. They're the same wherever you go. It's only within our community that you find any real tolerance. Our people aren't just one type—all sorts take to traveling, and some we'd rather hadn't, but we still accept them. Out there"—he waved an arm in a broad gesture to take in the rest of the world—"it's conform or suffer for it, let yourself be squeezed into their mold while you die inside, or live your life on the wrong side of a barrier of suspicion and hate."

Carla had heard it all before. Her father's tirade began to irritate her. She knew from her own experience that there was truth in what he said. But wasn't he just as prejudiced, in his own way? Not everyone "out there" was the same. She knew that, and so did he. It got them nowhere to withdraw into their own camp, and treat the rest of the world as aliens.

Jeanie listened with fascination to thoughts that were new to her. She knew what it was like to be an outcast.

She too had been ridiculed and rejected for being different, and through no fault of her own. She had only been able to cope by withdrawing, making her own private world in which she could survive. In a different way, the travelers had done the same thing. That must have been what had attracted her to them.

Jake, on the other hand, wasn't content with her way. The love he talked about so much was so important to him that he wanted everyone to live by it as he did—accepting one another and doing one another good. *Why did he care so much?* Jeanie wondered. In any case, was it really possible for Jake's "wind" to blow into other lives and change them? Even closed minds, if only they'd open the door? Something had happened to her, and now her mother. Was it just Jake, or was there really a wind blowing, something from outside them all?

Jake didn't argue with Chris. He leaned forward, holding out his long hands in urgent entreaty.

"This meeting tomorrow night is your opportunity to convince the village that you are people they can live beside. Let them see you close up, put faces and names to the bogeymen they've created for themselves. They'll see you're no different from them. Talk to them. Send four of you at most, so as not to alarm them. It would be risky. They may see it as an intrusion, but most of them are decent people; they believe in old-fashioned fair play, and they'd give you a hearing. If you withdraw behind barricades nothing can happen. Take a risk, and something good may come of it."

Chris and Angharad both shook their heads immediately and firmly.

"We've tried this kind of thing before," Angharad said."People are either for you or against you. Whatever you do, they interpret according to their prejudices. Some listen, but they are the ones who are already open. Those who aren't just feel more threatened—and they are always the majority."

She looked kindly at Jake as if he were a child who knew no better.

"We've lived this way a long time. It shocked us at first, the narrow-mindedness of people. Even eccentrics get some respect so long as they stay within certain bounds. I've always done as I pleased and not worried what people think of me, but the moment I went on the road with Chris, I saw people's attitudes change. For most of them, travelers are not human at all. We have no rights. We don't even pay tax. That's the thing they really hate. We're worth nothing because we pay nothing to the state.

"All you can do is learn to survive, just like the rest of the natural world. The rabbit doesn't try to convince the fox to become a vegetarian. It just stays in its burrow. It's the way things are."

"The only person around here who has ever given us the time of day," Jo put in, "is Bill Baines. And we never had to persuade him. He's just like that. He sees us as people and treats everyone the same. It's no good, Jake. You're far too idealistic. People don't respond to reason or even to gestures of friendship. They want things to stay as they are, so long as they're comfortable."

As she went on her voice shook.

"I know how far they'll go. I was there in the beanfield when they shut us out of Stonehenge. They herded us into a field, the police came in force and smashed the windows of our vans, turned us out, and beat us up. I was there. I'll never forget it, and I'll never trust any of them again."

Jo squeezed Pippin so protectively to her that he woke and cried. You could see in her face the terror and hatred of the day she spoke about. You could see it had never really left her.

The three of them stared at Jake, hostile. His was not the solution they wanted, and even in Jeanie's eyes it had seemed inadequate. Why expect people to change now, when they never had before?

Jake seemed to have shrunk into the depths of the chair, his eyes dull. As he pulled himself wearily to his feet his shoulders drooped. He seemed suddenly much older.

"As you wish," he said quietly. "I take it you'll be leaving, then, as soon as you can?"

Chris hesitated momentarily, reaching out a hand to Jake's shoulder. The man had turned out a disappointment, but he meant well. It was a pity to crush him.

"We'll just wait and see what happens tomorrow night," he said gently. "You never know—a miracle might happen."

Although she couldn't see his face in the darkness as they walked silently back towards the village, Jeanie could feel an oppression in Jake that was more than sadness. He walked as if every step was painful, as if with every part of him he did not want to go on. The love Jeanie felt for him, but could not express, hurt almost as much, filling her to bursting with the longing to take him in her arms and comfort him.

"Is there anything we can still do?" she asked timidly as they neared her home.

He gave a great sigh, as if trying to expel some burden she could not share, but then seemed to shake himself and remember she was there.

"Thanks for that 'we,' Jeanie. It's good to have such a loyal friend." He touched her lightly on the shoulder but withdrew his hand quickly.

"There are some things only I can do, my love."

He broke off short as if the words had been snatched away.

She found tears of pain and joy pricking her eyes, because of the name he had called her, but more because at this moment she felt she was closer to him than anyone else in the world.

"Could you go and see this Mr. Baines tomorrow and persuade him to come to the meeting?"

"Of course." She would have done anything, but this was easy.

They reached the gate of the bungalow. From behind closed curtains a warm glow of light spilled onto the neglected front garden. Mom was waiting for her. Home was home in a way it hadn't been until today. Jeanie's gratitude to Jake overflowed.

"Jake?" He looked down at her, still with that sad, shadowed look she felt she couldn't bear.

"What are you going to do? Will you be all right?"

He didn't answer straightaway. Then he took a deep breath, shook himself, and managed the ghost of his old smile.

"Happy are the peacemakers, Jeanie, for God will call them His children." He spoke with a peculiar emphasis, hanging on to every word as if to make it his own. Then he had turned abruptly away and was gone.

She stood transfixed, because other words were coming back to her from some lesson long ago. "Happy are those who are persecuted . . . Happy are you when people insult you and tell all kinds of lies against you because you are my followers . . ."

She was afraid for him. She could see he was afraid for himself, but would not turn away from what lay ahead.

At the same time she thought she was beginning, at last, to understand him.

The Village at Odds

18

The parish room was a "temporary building" of forty years ago, made of corrugated iron painted a faded shade of green. Corners of the metal sheeting had long since begun to rust away, allowing chinks of light to show here and there along the walls. It was too draughty to use in winter, and even after a dry summer the hall smelled musty and damp. Autumn was drawing in and the evening was chilly. Most of the villagers kept their coats on.

Mrs. Dillon had been in during the afternoon to sweep up. Disturbed dust particles still hung in the air and tickled the nose. She had even decorously covered the table at the front with a white cloth and put a vase of purple Michaelmas daisies on it. Behind it, the rusty black curtains covering a little stage once used for school concerts and Christmas pantomimes shivered in the scurrying drafts.

Three people sat behind the table. In the middle was Mr. Adamson, churchwarden, chairman of the Parish Council and Caroline's father. On his left, dwarfing him, Mr. Crocker the publican. On his right, Mrs. Palmer, busy writing headings in a hardbacked notebook.

Mr. Adamson was a slight, neat, balding man who

wore a suit instead of his usual comfortable cardigan, because he had only just had time for tea after traveling home from his job in town. He looked as if he had indigestion and wanted the meeting over as soon as possible. He scanned impatiently the fifty-odd villagers standing around chatting at the back while the rows of faded green canvas chairs stood empty, and banged on the table with a small wooden cube.

"Please come in and sit down," he called out in a tone that expected attention, surprisingly powerful for one so small. "It is almost half-past seven. The meeting will start on time."

People shuffled along the lines of chairs and sat down with a creaking and clashing of metal logs. Jeanie found a place at the back next to the Bentons, looking over her shoulder anxiously in the hope that Bill Baines would still turn up.

"I'll come if I can," he had said in his easygoing way. "If I can get this lot of potatoes bagged and ready for the truck in the morning."

It had been difficult to convince him how important it was, that there was no one else to speak up for the travelers. "It won't hurt them to cut their losses and clear out now," he had insisted. "Things will calm down over the winter and by next year everyone will have forgotten this bit of trouble. Don't worry about it so much. Besides, I doubt if anyone will listen to me. I've had my disagreements with them in the village before now. They don't think a lot of Bill Baines' opinions."

He had smiled at her kindly, and Mrs. Baines had given her tea and scones in the untidy kitchen, talking about

Chris and Angharad and how they had known them years ago, and what Carla had been like as a baby. Bill had put his boots up on the wooden coffee table with a wink at the half-serious face his wife pulled at him. Another day, Jeanie would have liked being there with their warmth and ease, but today she fidgeted restlessly, taut as a bow with the urgency of her mission, unable to put it into words. How could she explain Jake's insistence that they come, or describe the suffering in his eyes?

Mr. Adamson was again calling the meeting to order, lining up the edges of the small pile of papers in front of him with delicate touches of the fingertips, looking at the audience over the top of his half-moon glasses until they muttered into submission. He stood up, clearing his throat.

"The agenda is as follows. Mr. Crocker called this meeting and will begin by explaining his reasons for doing so. The meeting will then be open to the floor."

The publican shifted uncomfortably in his chair, un-crossing and crossing his massive forearms as if uneasy at not having a bar to rest them on. Mr. Adamson, glancing lightly to left and right, getting into his stride, went on.

"I am sure you would all wish me to thank Mrs. Palmer for kindly agreeing to take the minutes."

He smiled a small smile, and Mrs. Palmer looked coyly down at her notebook as one or two of the audience, out of habit, began to applaud, and stopped after the second clap. A tiny flutter of resignation brushed the rows of faces as Mr. Adamson glanced at his notes and carried on.

"I am sure you all know already about the appalling disturbance caused on Sunday evening by the vagrants who have camped themselves by the beach. I am sure we all feel that such people should not be allowed to remain. We are a small community and a quiet one. Disturbances such as this have never been known here before. We have the right to live peacefully and without the fear of violence. In addition, many of us depend on the visitors who value our isolation when they come for a holiday or a day at the seaside for our income. These interlopers could destroy not only our way of life, but also our livelihood. I take it there is no argument about whether these people should be made to go. The only question is, how is it to be done? I believe Mr. Crocker has a proposal to put to us."

Mr. Adamson inclined his neat head courteously to the companion on his left.

"Mr. Crocker."

He sat down. Mr. Crocker got to his feet slowly, towering over the little table with his six-feet and two hundred-pound frame. It was easy to see why the Black Lion was the most law-abiding pub for miles around. But in front of an audience, the big fellow was nervous. His friends knew him as a mild, shy man, for whom putting thoughts into words required great effort. He cleared his throat, perched a pair of reading glasses on his nose, and began unfolding a slightly grubby sheet of paper which he produced from the back pocket of his corduroy trousers.

"I should like to propose," he began solemnly, "that this meeting pass the following resolution." He cleared his throat again and read laboriously from the piece of paper.

"We, the residents and parish councilors of Sea Norton, object to the presence of persons of no fixed abode on land adjoining our village. These squatters are not only of no value to the community and contribute nothing to the cost of its services, they have also committed crimes against property and assaults on members of the police, as well as breaches of the peace. We request that they be removed immediately and brought to justice."

Mr. Crocker took a deep breath and looked around the meeting. "I suggest we all sign this and collect signatures from other people in the village, and send it to the District Council, the Chief Constable, and the Justices of the Peace. And anyone else we can think of. That's my suggestion."

He sat down abruptly and with evident relief. Mr. Palmer immediately sprang to his feet in the middle of the hall. A thin man with a long, thin face, he leaned forward, gripping the back of the chair in front, twisted like wire with the strength of his feelings.

"It's not enough!" he almost shouted. "What good d'you think it'll do? Where were the police on Sunday night? Where were the authorities?"

He looked around, willing the audience to follow his lead.

"Where were they? Not a policeman anywhere for miles! And who dealt with that lot?"

An answering murmur this time.

"That's right! We did! Les Crocker and Tom Benton and the rest of us. We sorted them out!"

Mr. Palmer's voice dropped almost to a whisper, and the hall was very quiet.

"If we want to be rid of these vermin we'll have to

flush them out and drive them away. There's no other way."

He sat down. For a minute or two the silence held. Then there was a rustle of movement. Those who had come to sit passively through the meeting took their hands out of their pockets and raised their chins from hunched shoulders. Next, a low buzz of talk. Then, taking courage, a rapid succession of villagers took the floor. One by one they brought up their grievances and polished them up. Petty thefts, vandalism, and outrageous behavior were described all over again. The pace grew faster. Everyone wanted a say. Mr. Adamson gave up trying to keep order as suggestions and countersuggestions flew back and forth.

"We should set the dogs on them."

"You should see the pack of fierce brutes they've got there."

"Call in the men from Pumpstead and Otterbury. We'd outnumber them by ten to one."

"Then what? D'you think that lot'd be frightened of us?"

"Take a few stakes and shovels with us. That'll soon frighten them."

"You'd have to start a riot first."

"Why not? Just so long as we get rid of them."

"We could go along at night and light a bit of a bonfire. That'd soon terrify them."

"Break a few more windows."

"I'd take my shotgun along."

At this appalling suggestion there was a momentary

silence, a collective intake of breath as even the boldest were alarmed by where their rhetoric was leading.

The pause allowed Tom Benton to get to his feet.

"Just a moment."

His voice was quiet but it carried so all could hear him. Everyone stopped talking. Most people listened when Tom Benton had something to say. They knew him and trusted him, the man who would take the lifeboat out and risk his life for yours. His slow, reasonable speech, pausing at every sentence end, acted like a cold shower.

"Just stop and listen to yourselves a minute. You're suggesting we take to violence. Take the law into our own hands. Who says these people are guilty? Not a court of law. This is a law-abiding village. We live in a law-abiding country—thank God. This is England—not the jungle. You sound no better than a pack of savages."

There was silence. People became suddenly absorbed in studying their hands, or the legs of the chair in front of them. Not Mr. Palmer. He was on his feet again, spitting out his words.

"Of course they're guilty. What about Michael Richardson's motorbike? Are you telling me they had nothing to do with that?"

Tom looked him straight in the eye.

"Do you have any proof?"

He looked confidently around the room.

"Does anyone else?"

No one answered.

"Or about any of the other things you accuse them of?

I notice no one called in the police to investigate. You'd all rather make up your minds without any facts to go on."

They were believing him now, letting themselves be swayed. *Good old Tom!* Jeanie thought, *They know he's right, he'll win them.* But then it struck her, coldly, how easily these people were led. They followed Tom now, but who would gain them in the end?

Tom, legs firmly planted as if on the deck of a ship, launched again into his arguments, repeating the same solid truths.

"I was the first at the camp on Sunday night," he went on, "and what I saw was an attack by a gang of louts in black leathers. There were women and children there, and the men were defending them. Did anyone else see that?"

He looked hard at Mr. Crocker, who grunted and gave half a nod. Then at Mr. Palmer, who avoided his eye.

"I'll admit the situation was confused, but that was what I saw. If you want to get rid of violence, you should look for those lads on bikes. As for the others, it doesn't bother me whether they go or stay, so long as what we do is legal. But I'll have no part in the sort of thing you're talking of. That's plain wrong, and those who suggest it are worse than vagrants."

He had gone too far. They didn't like it. Imperceptibly, the tide of feeling had begun to flow back the other way.

A Stranger in the Midst

19

There was a small lull after Tom sat down. People shifted in their seats and whispered to one another, but no one was ready for an open challenge. Jeanie felt a brief touch on her arm as Bill Baines passed her to slip into a seat in the row in front. Mrs. Palmer scribbled busily in her notebook

Then from the front row a tall figure unfolded itself. Dr. Richardson turned to face the meeting, his neat gray hair, his well-cut tweed suit all commanding attention from those who considered themselves just ordinary folk. Everyone sat up a little in expectancy. He spoke deliberately, his cultured tones cutting like cold steel.

"Thank you, Tom, for calling my son a lout," he began. Tom, overcome with embarrassment, blushed and looked at his feet. Hadn't the doctor brought his son into the world? Come out in the night when the baby gasped and struggled with croup? Everybody knew what a good man Dr. Richardson was.

The doctor turned his gaze from the Bentons and swept it over the rest of the gathering—his patients every one.

"I admit that Michael was in bad company on Sunday,

and got involved in an unfortunate prank. For which, I may say, he is being punished. You all know Michael—up to mischief from the day he was born."

He smiled indulgently, and the villagers, who had indeed known the blond little tyrant since boyhood, for the most part smiled with him.

Jeanie did not. Neither did Jim.

"My son tells me they never intended violence. A silly feud between two groups got a little out of hand. Finally the travelers attacked Michael and his friends. I have to admit, however, that the interpretation is open to doubt. Such situations can be very confused. Tom is right; we should not take on the functions of a court of law."

The doctor bowed slightly in Tom's direction. He began to sound like a lawyer setting out his case: reasonable, persuasive, his logic hard to fault.

"Whatever the rights and wrongs of that incident, I have something to tell you which I think may confirm the view some of you have already expressed about these unwelcome visitors. Something that happened yesterday afternoon."

He paused, enjoying the heightened interest he had aroused. He looked so distinguished, Jeanie thought, so handsome, so plausible. So like Michael, a cold thought came suddenly. He always gets his own way. He will win them back.

"Yesterday afternoon Michael was out on the dunes when he was viciously assaulted by a group of young men. He was attacked from behind and knocked almost senseless. Therefore, of course, he could not swear to their identities in a court of law, but he is convinced—and so am I—that they were from this so-called traveler community. He's not well enough to come tonight. I think even Tom will agree that the crime of causing actual bodily harm is one that cannot be ignored."

Jeanie's sharp intake of breath at Michael's lie was completely drowned in the uproar that followed. She looked around. Angry faces, open mouths, yells of indignation and hate. Some on their feet now, shaking fists. Some turning towards Tom Benton, scornful. All of them angry without cause, carried away by falsehood and their own fear and prejudice.

She alone knew what had really happened. Stand up, girl, tell them . . . How could she? She would be accusing Owen. Fair fight or not, he had still hurt Michael. She shrank down in her seat, wishing herself invisible, wishing herself anywhere but there. There was nothing, nothing she could do.

When Bill Baines stood up they all saw at once that he was angry, and all of them were shocked. Bill was never angry. Always laid back, casual, good-tempered. He never took sides in the minor feuds of village life. "It'll blow over," was always his attitude. "No point in making bad blood. Besides, there are two sides to every argument." His neutrality had won him few friends.

But now there was something terrible about him. With a tremendous effort he managed to speak, each word carrying the weight of his anger.

"Your son's a liar."

This to the doctor, who was stunned into silence. Then Bill turned to the rows of people in their chairs.

"I've known that family of travelers for fifteen years, and I've known Michael, too. I've no doubt which of them is more likely to attack unprovoked. My son went to school with Michael, and the boy always was a bully. You ask yourselves. You know it's true."

He took a deep breath, reigning in anger.

"None of you have so much as spoken to the travelers, yet you dare pass judgement on them. You assume they're criminals. If you knew anything about them, you'd know that Chris and Angharad—and that's the first time anyone has given them a name—have always been against violence of any sort. It's what they believe in. They would never go against that belief, any more than they'd settle in a house and get a job like ordinary people. They've brought their children up the same. They'll defend themselves and their home, but never—never—would they attack.

"That's more than I can say about your son, Dr. Richardson. If you're honest with yourself, you know it too. Michael was always a coward. If he was beaten, I'll lay odds it was in a fair fight."

Dr. Richardson took a step towards Bill, and Jeanie, seeing his clenched fist, thought for a moment he was going to hit Bill. But he bit back his anger and stood glaring through narrowed eyes. Bill could not have said anything to infuriate him more.

If the doctor had been able to speak no one would have heard him. Again the meeting was in uproar. Most of the people were on their feet. Chairs crashed to the floor as villagers hurled abuse at Bill Baines and at the travelers. One or two were beside the doctor, clapping him on the shoulder to assure him of their support. A woman was standing on a chair, screaming above the hubbub words that nobody could hear.

Someone was shaking his fist in Bill's face, yelling, features distorted like a horrid caricature, spraying spittle. Bill retreated, step by step. His back was to the wall, his face white and bewildered. Such hatred, how could he have stirred up such hatred? Only Jeanie sat still, and beside her Tom and Jim Benton, horrified, unable to move an inch.

"Get them out, get them out, get them out," a rhythmic chant began to emerge from the cacophony. First one or two, then more, then the whole assembly took up the words, stamping feet on the floor, hands on the table, a hideous drumbeat. Nothing would satisfy them, Jeanie knew with the sharp pain of despair, nothing but blood. Nothing could stop them now.

They had begun to form into ragged ranks, a motley army setting out to destroy. Some had picked up improvised weapons—walking sticks, pieces of furniture in forgotten corners. Others looked around vaguely as if expecting a missile or instrument of battle to come to hand, then turned towards the doorway, hopeful. Something would be found.

They were not thinking now. Instinct drew them, the animal urges of fear and self-preservation. Destroy the Other! Destroy the Other! The call would not be denied. Drawing together into a phalanx for battle, they headed for the door.

Their way was barred. A hand stretched from one doorpost to the other; motionless, watching, Jake stood on the threshold. His long coat swirled around his ankles in the night wind. Behind him the rising moon silhouetted his tall and extraordinary shape. A shiver went down Jeanie's spine, and with it a sob of relief and joy.

The rabble hesitated. Jake's stillness had a quality that no one dared break.

"I have seen what you are doing," Jake said quietly, and his words fell into a pool of silence that seemed to spread out into the room so suddenly that some stood with their mouths open in mid-shout. Jake's eyes, deep and wide, rested on each. They knew what he saw.

How long had he been there? Did he see what I did, did he hear the things I said? This stranger—this person—did he witness the explosion of my rage and hate? One by one their eyes left his face and searched for somewhere else to look.

All of this, too, Jake saw. His seeing eyes continued to look slowly around the room. They met Jeanie's, and smiled. Then Bill's, and Tom's, acknowledging. None of the rest could meet his gaze. The silence grew oppressive, but no one dared break it.

"You think yourselves wronged," he said at last, but not a single head nodded in agreement.

"For some of you that may be true," he went on, looking directly at Dr. Richardson, who had retreated, little by little, so far to the other end of the room that he stood under a green sign saying *Emergency Exit*.

"I understand your hurt," he said, and the doctor took a small step forward again. "But hurting in return will not make it any less.

"Some people say revenge is sweet. Don't believe

them. Believe me, it is poison and will destroy you. I am telling you the truth."

The quiet voice had steel in it now. Jake left the doorway and came into the body of the hall. Every eye followed him. Those who carried sticks looked around for ways to be rid of them. One or two sat down, but most remained standing, fascinated by the tall figure, the gaunt face, the fire in his eyes.

Jeanie had never seen Jake like this before. In glimpses she had seen in part this strange and powerful person. At the same time she knew the vulnerability that lay behind, the price he was paying. It was as if he had been gathering all his strength for this moment, and in her sympathetic heart she ached for him. This was a battle he had to win. He had to bring life and hope to her. If he failed, somehow or other he would be destroyed.

He was in the middle of them now.

"Let me tell you a story," he began. Still cautious, hesitant, they began to let him have his way. Jake's manner changed. He looked around at them affectionately, slipping into colloquial, breezy story-telling mode.

"I'm sure you all know how different children of the same family can be. Some are no trouble—they always do what they're told and make their parents proud of them. Others are nothing but a disappointment. I knew a family like that once. The two boys were like chalk and cheese. The elder one did well at school and ended up in the family business. The younger one would have nothing to do with it. He talked his dad into buying shares in a harebrained venture of his own, and lost the lot."

He told it so well, looking around and catching the

eye of first one, then another, that he had them now in the palm of his hand. The stranger was no longer a figure of fear. What he was talking about none of them could fathom, but something drew them to listen, even to trust.

"Well, Dads? What would you do?" One or two grimaced and shook their heads. He should tell them.

"Would you throw him out? Have nothing more to do with him? He's lost all your money, remember."

Some shrugged and looked at the ground. Jake looked directly at Dr. Richardson.

"You, sir. You have a son. Would you cut yourself off from him if he wronged you in that way?"

The doctor, still leaning solitary in the doorway, shifted uncomfortably but did not reply.

Jake smiled.

"Don't be ashamed of loving your children. Of course you wouldn't let anything in the world separate you from them. Whatever they do, you forgive them, because you don't want to lose them. It's the way of love. You all know that."

He stretched out his arms in a gesture that included everyone.

"You already know what forgiveness means. As parents you forgive, you have to. How much more you are forgiven by your heavenly Father. All you have to do now is forgive in your turn. These travelers may have wronged you—accept it. Everyone is liable to do wrong. Everyone needs forgiveness. Forgive them now. Hatred brings death and darkness. Love brings life. That is the Kingdom of Heaven. You must choose. There is no other way."

In the silence that followed Jeanie knew, looking around the circles of faces, that Jake had won.

Not that he had convinced them all. Some drank in his words, knowing in their heart of hearts that they were more true than anything they had ever heard. Others grudgingly admitted to themselves that he was probably right. Yet others resisted, but acknowledged that now it would be impossible to do what they had wanted—at least for the time being.

There was a shuffling of feet and clearing of throats, but no one could think of anything to say.

The door still stood open, allowing the chilly east wind to stir the papers on the chairman's table. Mr. Adamson rearranged them self-consciously, as if trying to find a way of re-establishing the authority of his position.

From outside came a sharp explosion, then the crash of breaking glass, and faintly, a single human cry.

Heads went up, hands went out as if each tried to restrain his neighbor.

Another cry—deep, full-throated, a cry of triumph.

Now they were all at the door. From the direction of the travelers' camp came more crashes, shouts, and the unmistakable scream of a terrified woman.

The alder trees by the dunes were silhouetted against an angry orange glow.

Fire!

20

Young David, playing up on the dunes in the dying light, was the first to notice anything amiss. Owen, coming back empty-handed from the evening check on his rabbit snares, found him flat on his stomach in the long grass at the seaward edge of the sandhills. Concrete sea defenses made an artificial cliff at this spot, and David's head craned out over the drop to see along the beach in the direction of the village slipway. Owen came on him unawares and gave him a brotherly poke in the ribs with his foot. Instead of yelling in protest, David writhed and grimaced, shushing with such serious intensity that Owen dropped to the ground at his side and peered over his little brother's shoulder.

Not ten yards away three men sat close in under the wall. From time to time their voices could be heard faintly above the sea sound, but not the words they were saying. Nor could the boys lean far enough out to see their faces as they sat with their backs propped against the wall—only three pairs of jean-clad legs, one wearing motorcycling boots, and the occasional glimpse of a leather or denim sleeve as a gesticulating arm swept out towards the sea.

"Do you think it's them?" David whispered voicelessly in Owen's ear.

"Can't tell. Could be. Those boots look like Skull."

David wriggled forward, bracing himself on his elbows, until his shoulders were level with the rasping concrete edge, risking discovery for a better angle until Owen, nervous, clumsily pulled him back.

"Ouch!" Rolling on his back, David was for a moment wholly occupied with the blood welling in droplets from his grazed elbow.

"Did you see?"

David nodded. "I'm sure it was him. The fat one. Not sure about the others. They had helmets on before."

"Go and tell Dad. Quietly."

"You don't have to tell me."

Proving the point with elaborate caution, the younger boy slid silently up the bank until he could safely get to his feet and pick his way delicately between the grass tufts and prickly clumps of sea holly. Owen turned back to consider his position. Could he edge closer? So long as none of them moved and he could not see their faces, they would not see him. The main danger was of giveaway trickles of sand.

An empty beer can, lobbed in the direction of the sea, gave him confidence to move. It seemed they were off their guard.

At five-yards distance he could hear their voices clearly, though so disjointed by gusts of wind and the variable crash and murmur of waves that the words made no sense.

"Bikes . . . village . . . getaway . . . cops . . ." Then raucous laughter.

He was about to give up when someone else joined the group. He dared not pull forward to take a look. He kept very still, ears straining for the slightest sound. A different voice, younger, lighter-sounding. An enthusiastic greeting. The voices dropped. Sounds of movement, of sand being brushed from clothing. Another beer can, thrown into the dunes this time, narrowly missing Owen's head. Scuffling footsteps. The voices gradually receding. Only then did Owen cautiously push his head through the grass to stare after the four receding figures. No doubt about it now. The silver-painted skull on the back of the big man's leather jacket stood out even in the near-darkness. And the fourth figure—limping slightly—was unmistakably that of Michael Richardson.

His voice floated faintly over his shoulder in a sudden lull in the surf.

"Dad's gone to this village meeting. And look what I've got!"

A small object tossed in the air glinted in the fading light. Owen was sure it was a key.

* * *

Angharad, squatting on her low stool as Tansy the goat peered around curiously to see why the milking had stopped, was holding David by both shoulders and looking earnestly into his face.

"You can't be altogether sure, can you, dear? You didn't see his face. It won't do to let fear run away with us. It could easily be anyone sitting down there under the wall. People do it all the time."

David's small, dark face was screwed up with determination, and he shook his head vigorously until his long forelock fell over his eyes. Brushing it back impatiently, he repeated:

"I know it was them. I saw them. I know them. It was them, Mom. Owen thought so too."

"It was them, Mom."

Owen had come up behind Angharad and startled her by speaking. She twisted to look up at him, angry at being surprised, angry because she was wrong, and because what she had feared was true.

"They've gone back towards the slipway now. I saw them clearly. And the other one, the boy Jeanie knows, came to get them. I heard them talking. They mentioned bikes and police. I'm sure they're up to no good."

Angharad turned back to squeeze the goat's willing teats, squirting milk into the bucket regularly and skillfully, working herself under control. Tansy felt the tension in her hands and shifted uneasily.

"Chris isn't back. We heard there's another bus up the coast. He went on the bike to see who it was and whether it'd be better if we moved up where they are. He's been gone two hours."

"Don't worry, Mom. There's me and Phil and Gary." Owen, in spite of his slight build, almost visibly drew his father's mantle around him. He would protect the family now.

"There are only four of them, and we won't be surprised. We'll fix wires all around, just in case, but they may not come on their bikes. From what I heard I think they're keeping them for a getaway."

Owen put a hand on his mother's shoulder, but Angharad brushed it off impatiently, getting up with the full bucket of milk in her hand. Owen persevered. Guilt told him that now he could redeem himself.

"Dad's probably found they're friends and stayed to catch up on news. You know how he is. Don't worry. That bunch may be here for something quite different. Nothing to do with us. We'll be OK."

But his face, as he went to rouse Gary and Phil, told a different tale.

Angharad lifted the bucket stiffly and looked after him anxiously.

"Owen!"

He turned back.

"Don't do anything rash. Or those two." She nodded in the direction of the battered khaki tent. "I don't trust them," she said softly so that Owen would not hear. "And don't forget to warn Jo."

"Tether Tansy under the tree," she told David, turning back to the bus. Best to get the little ones into bed. They were safest inside, especially now that the windows were mostly boarded up. Not much could happen to them there.

Carla had raised her voice as she told Gwen her bedtime story so that the little girl would not hear the conversation outside. She hugged her close, all warm and sleepy as she was, and carried her to her bunk. Then with the partition closed behind her, she turned to face Angharad in the lamplight.

"We'll be safe inside," Angharad said aloud. "We can barricade the door and windows. If they can't get in, they can't hurt us, can they?"

They both wanted her to be right. Determinedly, they found busywork, Angharad setting out her lace pillow, Carla carefully choosing a book.

"Tansy's settled down. I moved the chicken coop under the trees, too."

David climbed on to the bus, his square little body proud with grown-up responsibilities.

"Jo says she'll come over when Pippin's asleep. She wasn't worried. She says she'll give them as good as she gets. She's got a few things to throw if she needs them. Owen wants me to help him."

He turned and went out again with a torch. Carla smiled at his retreating back. Jo was probably right. She was quite capable of scaring the living daylights out of any attackers. Her confidence was warming. What could they do, after all? They weren't going to be murdered in their beds.

In half an hour darkness had completely closed in. It was quiet. Slowly they began to relax. The threat, after all, was only a threat. Perhaps nothing would happen, like last night. Angharad finished pinning a new section of pattern and yawned.

"Time that boy was in bed."

A shout froze her in her place. Then another, from the opposite side. A crashing of branches. A cacophony of whoops and yells from every direction. They were all around, and closing in like hunters on their prey. How many of them? More than four, for certain—far more. A loud explosion catapulted Carla and Angharad into each other's arms, and then Gwennie was there, worming terrified to a safe haven between their bodies.

David was in the doorway, white-faced but brave.

"It was only a firework."

"They're trying to frighten us."

More noise, yells getting louder, sticks beating the undergrowth, nearer now. A thud as something hit the roof. Then a hail of missiles. Gwennie shrieked and Carla held her tighter. David was struggling with the door, but it would not shut.

Angharad was going to help him when a brick crashed through the windscreen, showering them all with fragments of glass and knocking the lamp to the floor. Carla grabbed at it, burning her hands as flame licked out and caught the rug, running along the floor towards Gwen in her long nightie. Gwen screamed, high-pitched, deafening, on and on. Carla went through the flame to get her, beating at the little fire that had begun to lick at the bottom of the child's skirts, running for the door.

Angharad had picked up the burning rug and was beating at the spreading flames.

"Mom! Get out!" Carla screamed and tripped backwards over the bus steps, clutching her awkward bundle of sobbing child, and hit the cold ground with a force that jerked the breath from her body.

Circle of Darkness

21

Jeanie pushed her way through the whipping alder and willow twigs, panting, scratched and weak with the fear of what she might see when she reached the camp. Heat from the flames reached her before she could properly see the bus ablaze. By the flickering orange light of the flames licking around the gaping windows, a crowd of people surged aimlessly back and forth. There were noise, shouts, excited talk. Jeanie pushed her way past one person after another, searching for Carla, Angharad, any of the friends who must be here somewhere.

"Has anyone phoned the fire brigade?" someone called out.

Nobody was sure.

"I'll run back to the village."

It was Jim, disappearing down the track at a rapid trot.

"Too late by the time they come."

"Ambulance, too, Jim, we need an ambulance," a voice yelled urgently after the boy, redoubling Jeanie's fear. She pushed her way in the direction of the voice, but wherever she turned, bodies moved and closed the way ahead.

"Get back!" someone was shouting. "Please get away from the fire."

Someone found a bucket of water and threw it at a tongue of flame licking greedily out of one of the broken, smoke-blackened windows. The flame disappeared with a hiss, then moments later sprang back, growling larger with every passing moment. The heat of the flames began to drive people backward. The fire found a voice, a deep, terrifying roar. Paint bubbled and spat, glass cracked, acrid smoke swirled into the spectators' eye and drove them farther down the clearing, up the dune, Jeanie with them. The crowd steadied and stilled, a mass of sober faces flicked by the light and darkness of the fire's uneven glow.

Sweat ran down Jeanie's face and into her eyes as she stared into the inferno. Surely they couldn't be in there? Nobody seemed to know, even to care. Sobs of despair rose in her throat as she pushed again at the standing bodies, trying to find her friends.

"Make a bucket chain! Get sea water!"

"Too late for that. There's nothing we can do."

"The woman says there's no petrol to worry about."

"Thank God for that."

There! At the base of the slope a knot of people stood around someone lying on the ground. Jeanie broke into a trot, straight for them, fear knotting her throat. Elbowing unceremoniously between two women, she stared down at the still figure stretched on the ground. It was Angharad, eyes closed, blue-lidded, face gray and still, looking smaller, more fragile than ever. But breathing.

Carla sat on the ground with her mother's head on her

lap. Gwennie clung to her, her fists clamped tightly around her sister's arm and her face buried in her shoulder. Jeanie crouched beside them, relief bringing tears. Carla spoke without turning, her hands moving mechanically, stroking Angharad's tangled hair away from her eyes.

"She tried to put the fire out. Then the smoke got too much and she couldn't get out. I had to drag her. I think she banged her head."

Carla coughed painfully, putting up a hand on which the burns stood out red and beginning to blister. She was shivering. Jeanie took off her coat and put it around Carla and Gwen. The night air felt damp. A mist was coming in from the sea.

Someone brought cold water for the burns. Only then did they notice the charred hem of the little girl's nightie and the red weals on her ankles. The child's pain seemed to stir a buried compassion in the onlookers. Warmth came into voices which until then had sounded stiff with the awkwardness of the evening's extraordinary changes of mood.

"The doctor's on his way."

"Poor little thing."

"No, don't try to take her away. She's terrified, can't you see? What a dreadful experience for a little girl."

Gwen was too frightened to accept comfort from strangers. She buried her face in Carla's smoke-blackened sweater, tugging at it to pull it over her ears too, to shut out the alien sights and sounds she did not want to hear.

Someone brought a blanket and they gently moved Angharad away from the fire. Suddenly the contagion of kindness spread. They competed to be kind, concerned, tender even, those people who only a short while before had been baying for the travelers' blood. Yet none of them, apart from Jeanie, spoke directly to the three, but only about them, over their heads, as though they wouldn't understand the language.

Dr. Richardson arrived with his emergency bag.

"I've called an ambulance."

He knelt briskly beside the casualties, efficient hands touching, eyes moving from faces to injured parts, assessing, doing his job, face giving nothing away. Only the stiff jerkiness of his movements, the brusqueness in his voice, which long practice could not quite hide, showed how difficult it was for him to be there.

At last Jeanie's senses, released from complete absorption in her hurt friends, began to be able to take in the pandemonium around her. Most of the crowd had turned away from the fire now. The action was elsewhere. It seemed to her that first she felt the tension, the fear, almost the smell of it, in spite of the foul smoke gusting across the dunes. Then sounds, sounds which knotted her innards with alarm. A confusion of hollow drumming, of shouts hoarse with a fierce excitement, of engines revving, receding, accelerating. Then an explosion, close by. She cowered, hands over ears. Almost on hands and knees she pushed her way through feet and legs, compelled to face whatever it was, unable to turn away.

A motorbike roared past, scattering indignant people. Then another. Two of them circling, no lights on, their masked riders sinister as they came into the fireglow and disappeared again towards the trees. Again Jeanie pushed urgently through resistant bodies, to be thrust back by the blast of noise and air as the bike came around again.

It was dark in the middle of the circle, where Jo's van stood surrounded. A forest of upraised arms stood out against the faint lightness of the sky. Arms in incessant, rhythmic movement, fists hammering on the van's roof and sides. Faceless visors, upturned, reflecting the flickering light of the blaze, emitted chilling, inhuman cries. They were like a pack of wolves closing on their prey, ready to tear it limb from limb. They were purposeful, united, intent on destruction. Jeanie stood rooted to the spot, cold to the core with horror. Without doubt, now she knew what Jake had meant when he talked about evil. It was not just the circling outriders who made the villagers hesitate to go closer. They too could see what he saw, and they were terrified of what had been unleashed.

There were unmasked faces among the faceless ones. Was that Owen, clinging to the step of the driver's door? Whoever it was, he was slashing furiously with a piece of driftwood at a knot of the dark-clad figures, similarly armed. They seemed about to overwhelm him when another joined him,—Gary? Phil?—clambering on the bumper to get the advantage of height, laying about him furiously. Then another, yelling like a banshee, a four-foot log whirling furiously about his head, to stand alongside the other two. But they were hopelessly outnumbered. They would never hold out against so many.

Where was Jo? And baby Pippin? Jeanie gasped aloud. They must be in the van. They were the quarry whose blood the pack were howling for. She could see them so clearly in her mind's eye, crouching terrified against the windows, those features distorted with hate, those fists crashing again and again on the glass.

Her hands clenched so hard that her nails bit into her palms. Do something, someone, do something. She was on her feet now, looking for someone who would fight for her. Les Crocker stood behind her, and she was pulling at his arm, begging, screaming until his great hands took her by the shoulders and shook her into submission.

"We tried, littl'un, we tried to get them off. But then they got the bikes going. We can't do anything, they're too many. The police'll be here soon, don't you worry. When they come we'll stop them. Till then, best to keep things calm, not aggravate them too much. They're not harming anyone just now."

"But the baby! There's a girl and a baby in there! They'll be scared stiff! You can't just stand and watch them!"

"Nothing we can do. Not just yet. Wait. It'll be all right, you'll see."

A crescendo of noise drowned his voice. Still gripping Jeanie's shoulder as if to restrain her from throwing herself into the fight, Les turned back to the fray. A change was coming. Out of the discordant chaos of sound a pattern was emerging, a rhythm which slowly grew and dominated, a hoarse shout coming and going, accelerating, exulting. Clinging like parasites, hands reaching up, pushing, pulling, in growing unison. They had begun to rock the van.

The onlookers stirred. Above the chant, for the first time the baby's cries came faintly. Men looked at one another. The impulse to protect the weak stirred strongly in them. Some took a step forward, then another. The crowd closed in, uncertain what to do. Some called out.

"That's enough now."

"You'll cause a real injury."

"Stop it!"

Jeers and catcalls answered them over leather-clad shoulders. The guarding bikes put on more speed, circling tighter, more dangerously. Still nobody dared break the circle.

The rocking went on, quickening in tempo. Now, at each push, a wheel left the ground. Then the van tipped farther, teetering, moving towards the point of equilibrium. The crowd seemed paralyzed, not believing what it saw. The chant grew more furious, wild, almost joyful—terrifying. And above it, Jo screamed.

At last the men threw caution to the wind. They burst through the ring of moving metal, oblivious to danger. As one man they were fighting, struggling to stop the worst from happening. Owen had leapt from the step and was locked in combat with one of the attackers. Other wrestling pairs broke away and fought their private battles with grunts and groans of triumph. Still the van rocked. Jeanie wanted to shut her eyes but could not. She stared transfixed, foreseeing with a wrenching that tore through her the awful thing that was going to happen. Forward, back, forward, back. It would fall towards the trees. They knew it, now. Those on the far side were loosening their hold, preparing to leap to safety as it fell. The rhythmic shout grew to a cry of exaltation.

Suddenly the back doors flew open and there was Jo,

a wild thing, hair flying, eyes staring, Pippin clutched to her chest. In one desperate leap she was clear of the van, out among the startled defenders, reached out to by protecting arms, sobbing, shaking, incoherently gesticulating towards the van which crashed back on one set of wheels, only to be caught and pushed again with a wild elated shout.

The attackers, startled, fell back. But the van had reached the point of no return. Alone, it stood for a moment balanced, teetering on two wheels, for a split second motionless. Then with a groan and a great clatter of falling objects within, the heavy body pulled it slowly, slowly down towards the ground.

"Jake!"

In that moment she saw him, his white exhausted face, his hands clinging desperately to the bodywork, spread-eagled, legs braced, arms outstretched, on the wrong side of the van.

Jeanie was running, running, restrained by firm and friendly hands, then losing control, shaking, falling, falling into the familiar sick blackness, lost.

But before she lost consciousness she had seen what they all saw, horrified. As the van fell with a crashing clangor, Jake was engulfed in the dark.

Footmarks in the Sand

22

Waking, Jeanie's senses were confused by quietness. Her dreams had been full of violent splinters of noise and color, the orange glare of flame and choking swirl of smoke, the black silhouettes of running figures, shouts, screams, curses. The circling flash of a blue beacon, the wail of sirens, hands lifting, voices gentling, a journey, an arrival . . . or had that been a waking dream?

"Mom?"

She tightened her fingers and found a warm, familiar hand holding hers. That part, at least, had been real. She lay for a while not moving, feeling the comfort flowing up her arm and melting the tightness in her body. It was very quiet. Somewhere, far away, footfalls and hushed voices drifted. Here was a white hospital ceiling, a pool of lamplight, a faint crack of dawn light edging the moment, knowing that soon her mind would soak up the pain that hovered on its fringes, and she would know why she was frightened to remember. She wanted to stay here in the womblike quiet, to close her eyes and sleep again . . .

Jake.

Now the scene replayed itself cruelly in her mind. She

saw the crucified figure stretched out across the van's side as it balanced, tottered, leaned, fell. She was helpless, she could do nothing to save him, her love was dying, was overwhelmed in that explosive, obliterating crash. No one could have survived that fall.

Jake was dead. Inside her, an unbearable black hole, a fathomless emptiness. Tears flowed from beneath her closed lids and ran down to make puddles in her ears. Tears without end, pain without end, life without Jake.

Mom's arms came around her, pressed her close. Hurt and grief burst out of Jeanie in tearing sobs, on and on while Mom rocked and held her and wept a little in sympathy. A nurse came in and looked, putting a hand on Jeanie's shaking shoulders.

"Let her have a good cry."

Her voice was homely, full of the experience that even pain that breaks a world apart will one day heal over and become history.

Mom nodded agreement over the heaving shoulders.

"She needs it."

Later, when the storm had subsided to an aching weakness, Jeanie leaned on Mom's shoulder and listened to her make some sense of her fractured recollections.

"I'm so sorry, dear. Jake was dead when they got the van off him. It would have been very quick. They said a fractured skull. Jo and Pippin are fine, they got out just in time. If they hadn't . . . He was shouting to her through the window, you see, telling her to jump, but she was too frightened. She could only see the gang, she didn't know there were other people there to help her once she was out. It was only as the van began to fall that she knew she had to go, and by then it was too late for Jake."

They were quiet together for a while.

"Jake gave his life for Jo and Pippin," Jeanie said softly at last. "And only the night before she'd told him to get lost. She didn't even like him much. He believed in love, Mom. And in good overcoming evil. And that was where it led him in the end. It doesn't seem to make sense."

"Greater love has no one than this," Mom quoted slowly, thoughtfully, recalling words learned long ago, "that he lay down his life for his friends."

Jeanie pulled away abruptly, tears welling up again to choke her. Suddenly she was angry—angry with Jake for dying, for throwing his life away when he could have stayed with her, when she needed him.

A futile gesture, a wild romantic demonstration which made no difference to anything. What was the point, when the hate that killed was so much more powerful than Jake and his love?

Yet, remembering Jake, she knew that was not really true. If she could only hold on to this . . .

* * *

Jeanie looked up at the sea of faces and tried to gain control of her voice.

"The lesson," she began again, "is from the Gospel according to St. John, chapter fifteen, beginning at the ninth verse."

There they all were, row by row, filling the church to the back doors. Not for years had so many turned out for a funeral. And she, Jeanie, knew every one of them:

Adamsons, Palmers, Bentons, Crockers, and—she glanced at the corner of the aisle— Chris, Angharad, Carla, Owen, and all the other travelers.

At their center was the plain wooden coffin with its single bunch of wildflowers that she and Carla had gathered in the hedgerows that morning. Bryony and clematis, poppy and corn marigold, campion and sea pink, the flowers Jake had talked about with such love so few days ago. Jeanie turned back to the faces in front of her before grief choked her again. So many faces. Most of them had hardly known him. But this once, Jake had brought them all together.

Jeanie looked down at the lectern again, forcing her eyes to focus on the words on the page of the open Bible.

"As the Father has loved me, so have I loved you."

She read slowly and clearly, putting meaning into every word because she wanted them all to understand. Her light voice shook a little from time to time. The congregation grew very quiet.

"Now remain in my love. If you obey my commands, you will remain in my love, just as I have obeyed my Father's commands and remain in his love. I have told you this so that my joy may be in you and that your joy may be complete. My command is this: Love each other as I have loved you. Greater love has no one than this, that he lay down his life for his friends."

She closed the book and went back to her place beside Mom. She knew, now, what it was that Jake had never been able to put into words that she would understand. She understood why he had done what he did. She could even, almost, accept that there was no other way for him, that dying had been a part of being true to himself, that the Jake she loved could have done nothing else.

She had read all about it, chapter by chapter, as she searched for the words she wanted, the ones she had just read aloud. She had read about the other One who had died, too, out of love for his friends, and his enemies too, and seen that it was He whom Jake had been following and His love that he had talked about. She wanted, more than anything else, to follow in the same way, because, though it frightened her, its beauty drew and held her irresistibly.

They stood up and sang, knelt and prayed, then carried Jake outside and laid him in the ground under the old churchyard trees.

Afterwards, most of the village drifted away.

"Jeanie?"

It was Angharad, a little paler than usual, her voice still hoarse from inhaled smoke. Beside her Carla had her hands swathed in bandages.

"Will you come back with us? We're leaving tomorrow. We'd like to say good-bye properly. And to your mother, too."

They walked together, slowly, down the beach road to the dunes, past the rustling reedbed and through the alders. For the last time, Jeanie thought sadly. In just a few days the most important thing in my life has sprung up and grown and come to fruition, and tomorrow it will be as if nothing had happened at all.

But her mood changed when she saw the traveler camp. It bustled with astonishing activity. The blackened wreckage of the old bus had gone, leaving only an oily stain on the sand. Who had found them a new one she didn't know, but she knew the people who had rapidly changed their funeral suits for overalls and were hard at work ripping out the old seats and converting it for traveler use. Tom Benton—no surprise there. Les Crocker—he had always been a good-natured man. But Mr. Adamson, looking a lot more relaxed, with a saw in his hand, than she had ever known him. And others, responding gladly to Chris' direction, as if they had never shouted for his blood just a few days before. *Were they so easy to change,* Jeanie wondered skeptically, *would they change back again before many more days passed?* Nevertheless, here they were, doing things they wouldn't have dreamed of doing—before.

"Will you come back next summer?" she asked Carla, when she had had time to take it all in. They were up on the dune slope, side by side, out of the way of the workers.

"I think we'll have to. We've got so many friends here." Her voice shook with incredulous laughter.

It was true. Village families had taken them in the night of the fire, and being homeless, they had stayed ever since. Of course there were some who still kept a suspicious distance. The Palmers could not manage more than neutrality. But the young couple who offered a bed to Jo and Pippin had become fast friends with her. Jo, in fact, was staying on until she could find a new van.

On the track beyond the trees a long silver car slid to a halt. The tall figure of Dr. Richardson unfolded from the driver's seat and came across the site, carrying his doctor's bag.

"You'd better let me have a last look at those hands, Carla. I hear you're off tomorrow."

He squatted beside them, unwinding the bandages until they could see the purpling weals running across Carla's fingers where she had tried to retrieve the burning lamp. Jeanie watched the face absorbed in the work, the strong skillful fingers, so careful to avoid hurting. It was funny how she had stopped being in awe of him, these last few days, now that she understood his weaknesses. And at the same time, she could appreciate that in his work, he had his own way of loving.

"How's Michael?" she asked.

The doctor flinched as if she had struck him. Then, with great effort, answered her shortly, but without putting up the blinds. He, too, had been learning these past few days.

"They refused bail. The charge is manslaughter. He'll be tried in the county court with the others. It could be some time. Until then he'll be in a remand center." He hesitated a long time, then said quietly, "My wife is very upset."

And so am I, it was his way of saying, but Jeanie knew better than to say so.

"I'm sorry."

"Thanks, Jeanie." He was fastening the fresh bandage, finishing it neatly, tucking in the ends. He looked up, gazing straight into her face. It seemed to cost him a great effort to speak.

"Jake was right, you know," he said. "I wish I'd listened to him before it was too late." He was packing his things away neatly in his bag, and she couldn't see his face as he went on almost inaudibly, almost speaking to himself.

"I realized that night that evil is not an outdated idea. And if it's real, then we have to fight it, whatever the cost. As Jake did."

He paused. "He was a remarkable man."

When he had gone, the girls climbed farther, to the top of the dune, and stood together looking out to the sea. *This is where it all started,* each of them was thinking, *this is where I came the day I first met Jake, this is where I was when I watched Jeanie dancing in the waves. Such a short time ago, yet it seems like years. The tides have come up and gone down, the season has begun to turn, everything changes. Jake came and now he is gone.*

A line of footsteps tracked across the wet sand where the tide would come up and obliterate them, soon, forever.

But the marks Jake left aren't like that, Jeanie told herself fiercely. *He may be gone, and soon we won't see where he came and went. But every grain of sand pressed down by the mark of a foot is minutely and invisibly changed. Jake left his mark on us. We won't be the same again—even though the tide will always be there, trying to wash the marks away.*

"Come on." Jeanie slipped her arm through Carla's and turned her round to face the busy camp again. "I think it's time we made the workers a cup of tea."